The Bite Before Christmas

Lynsay Sands
&
Jeaniene Frost

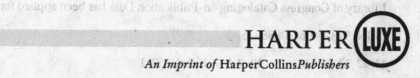

An Imprint of HarperCollinsPublishers

"THE GIFT." Copyright © 2011 by Lynsay Sands. "HOME FOR THE HOLIDAYS." Copyright © 2011 by Jeaniene Frost.

FIRST HARPERLUXE EDITION

HarperLuxe™ is a trademark of HarperCollins Publishers

Library of Congress Cataloging-in-Publication Data has been applied for.

ISBN: 978-0-06-208866-6

11 12 13 14 ID/OPM 10 9 8 7 6 5 4 3 2 1

ALSO BY LYNSAY SANDS

The Reluctant Vampire The Accidental Vampire

Hungry for You   Bite Me If You Can

Born to Bite   A Bite to Remember

The Renegade Hunter Tall Dark & Hungry

The Immortal Hunter Single White Vampire

The Rogue Hunter   Love Bites

Vampire Interrupted A Quick Bite

Vampires Are Forever

ALSO BY JEANIENE FROST

One Grave at a Time Destined for an Early Grave

This Side of the Grave At Grave's End

Eternal Kiss of Darkness One Foot in the Grave

First Drop of Crimson Halfway to the Grave

Contents

The Gift
by Lynsay Sands

One

Teddy woke up to find himself burrowed under the covers like a mole dug into the ground . . . and cold, which was unusual. He normally kicked off his blankets rather than burrowed, and he never woke up cold.

The heat must have gone off in the night, he realized. Tossing the blankets aside, he sat up and peered around the room. Stark sunlight was pouring through the window. It made it easy to see the cloud of mist that formed in front of his mouth with each exhalation.

Oh yeah, the heat was definitely off, he thought with a grimace and quickly slid out of bed. The carpet was cold underfoot as Teddy hurried up the hall. It opened into the main room at the end, a combination living room and kitchen/dining room. The left side was the carpeted living room area with a sofa, two chairs, a fireplace, and entertainment unit. The right side was a tiled kitchen and dining space.

Teddy's eyes automatically sought out the digital clock on the stove as he moved to the wall thermostat, but he paused when he saw its blank face. His eyes then shot to the DVD player on the television, but it, too, was blank. Teddy was pretty sure what was wrong, by this point, but couldn't resist flicking on the light switch at the end of the hall, just to be sure. He wasn't surprised when nothing happened. It wasn't just the heat that was off, but the power itself. There was no juice at all.

"Great," he muttered with disgust and hurried back to the bedroom. It was cold in the cottage and likely to get colder, at least until the problem with the power was fixed, which meant he was wasting precious body heat standing around barefoot in his flannels. He needed to dress quickly, pull on his outerwear, and head some- where warm to call Marguerite and find out whom he should contact about the power.

His suitcase sat on a chair in a corner of the bed- room he'd chosen. Teddy lifted the lid and grabbed the thickest pair of socks he'd packed, and then grabbed a second pair for good measure. He started to turn away, intending to sit on the bed to don the socks, but paused as his gaze slid out the window.

It had been dark when he'd arrived last night, and Teddy had marveled at how beautiful it all was as his headlights slid over the ice-encased branches of the trees and the deep snow on either side of the cleared driveway. It had all sparkled under his pickup's headlights like precious jewels. It wasn't such a grand sight now, he decided, as he peered at what had to be at least two feet of fresh snow on the driveway and yard. His pickup was now a small snow hill beside the cottage.

"Damn," he breathed and then returned to the matter at hand as his brain revised what had to be done. Dress warmly, find a shovel, dig his truck out of the driveway, and then head to town to find someplace warm with coffee and food, where he could call Marguerite in comfort.

Or maybe he should try to call Marguerite first, Teddy thought as he finished with his socks and dragged on jeans and a sweater over his flannel pajamas. It was going to take a hell of a long time to dig his way out of the driveway. By that time, whoever was supposed to fix the power might be here if he called before starting.

Deciding that was the better plan, Teddy finished dressing and headed out into the kitchen to find his phone. He'd plugged it in to charge before going to bed last night. Unfortunately, the power must have gone out shortly after that, because the battery was even lower now than when he'd plugged it in. The warning that the battery needed recharging was all he could get before it shut itself off.

Muttering under his breath, Teddy shoved it in his pocket, dragged on his coat, scarf, and boots, then grabbed his gloves and opened the kitchen door. If he thought the cottage was cold, the mudroom was positively frigid, and Teddy grimaced as he stepped into it. He didn't slow, however, but tugged on his gloves, grabbed the shovel leaning against the wall, and headed outside.

The moment he stepped off the deck he was knee-deep in snow. Teddy trudged through the flaky snow to the driver's side of the pickup, leaned his shovel against the truck, and then brushed away the snow until he could find the door handle. He had some thought of starting the pickup, plugging his phone in the car charger, and turning on the heat and defrost so that the windows could thaw out while he shoveled the driveway. But he'd locked the truck's doors last night and the lock was now frozen . . . and the de-icer was in the glove compartment, where he'd tossed it while packing the vehicle for the trip. Not terribly bright of him to forget to bring it in last night, he acknowledged with a sigh.

"This just isn't your day," Teddy muttered to himself as he turned to glance toward the road. The driveway was narrow and wound through the trees, which was great for privacy, but it was also long, which was terribly inconvenient now. It would take hours to shovel the way clear himself. Fortunately, he was hoping he wouldn't have to do more than clear off the pickup and a bit around it. Marguerite had said the county cleared the roads and there was a handyman who cleared the driveway and took care of other matters for the Willan sisters, who owned the cottage he was renting.

Hopefully, by the time the road was clear and this handy feller could get in to clear the driveway, the door lock would be thawed enough that he could get the door open. Teddy supposed the best thing he could do was fetch some firewood from the shed, start a fire in the cottage's fireplace, and warm up while he waited.

But some coffee would sure go nice with that fire, he thought and glanced toward the road again, wondering what the problem was with the power. Never one to sit around and wait on being rescued, Teddy started up the driveway. He'd just take a look and see what the situation was. If the road was clear, he'd go back, build a fire, and wait for the handyman to show up. If it wasn't . . . well, he hoped it was.

It seemed to take forever to make his way to the road. By the time he reached the end of the drive, Teddy was sweaty and panting. His knees were also acting up and complaining over the walk, something they wouldn't have done forty or even twenty years ago. Getting old kind of sucked, he thought grimly as he surveyed the road, noting that it hadn't been cleared yet. At least it hadn't been cleared all the way to the cottage. The road twisted out of sight just ten feet from where he stood.

Sighing, he considered what to do. His stomach was gnawing with hunger, his legs aching from trudging through the snow, his mouth was dry, and while he was hot and sweaty under his clothes, his face was beginning to burn with the cold. Teddy readjusted his scarf to give his face more protection against the low temperatures and then forced himself to continue on. Another ten feet, he told himself. He'd just walk to the bend, take a look up the road, and then head back to the cottage and build a fire.

Once he reached the bend, Teddy almost wished he hadn't made the effort. The sight of the white-coated road stretched out before him was a truly depressing thing. Not only wasn't it shoveled, but one look was enough to tell him that it wasn't likely to be for a while. Either there had been a fierce wind with the snow the night before, or the heavy snowfall had been too much for a couple of the older trees. Two had fallen that he could see: one just ten feet past the bend where he stood and another farther up the road. They would have to be shifted before the snow-removal vehicles could clear the road to his driveway.

They were also the reason the power was out, Teddy noted as he saw the downed lines the first tree had taken out. That wasn't going to be a fast fix. It was looking like he'd be without power for a bit . . . if he stayed, he thought with a sigh. Maybe once the trees were removed and the road was cleared, he should just turn around and start the six-hour trip back to Port Henry.

The thought was a depressing one. It was two days before Christmas, a time of year when Teddy tried to avoid Port Henry. It was why he was up here at the cottage in the first place. Back home, everyone knew he had no family to spend Christmas with and everyone invited him to theirs. If he was in town, he'd have to accept one of those invitations and then attend as the charity case, not really belonging but there out of the goodness of their hearts. The thought was a depressing one.

Shaking his head, he turned to start back only to pause as he spotted a figure in the trees on the other side of the driveway to his own cottage. The individual wore a bright red ski suit and stood as still as a stone, staring from the shadows of the trees. Bundled up as the person was, it was hard to tell for sure if it was a woman or a slender man or youth, but that didn't trouble him as much as the absolute stillness. There was something about it that made the hair on the back of his neck prickle nervously, and then the person pushed back the hood to reveal a fresh-faced young blonde with a bright smile.

"Hello. You must be my neighbor," she greeted cheerfully, moving forward.

"Looks like," Teddy agreed and felt a grin claim his own lips. As he moved to meet her halfway in the deep snow, he nodded toward the driveway they stood in front of. "I rented the Willan cottage here for the holidays."

"And I'm in the one next door." She jerked a gloved thumb back the way she'd come. "My cousin, Decker's."

Teddy looked curiously the way she'd gestured, able to make out a large cottage through the leafless trees. Glancing back to her, he smiled wryly. "Looks like we picked a bad time to be up here."

She chuckled at the suggestion and shook her head. "A little snow never hurt anyone. They'll clear it away quick enough."

"I'm not so sure," Teddy said with a sigh. "There are a couple of trees down. One took out the power line. It'll be a while before they get that cleared up."

"Damn," the blonde breathed, her smile fading to be replaced with concern. "Someone was supposed to be bringing me . . . provisions," she ended quietly.

"Then we're in the same boat," Teddy said wryly. "I intended to stop at a grocery store on the way in myself, but I mucked about at the Bass Pro in Vaughan and then a couple of those antiques places on the way up and got here so late I decided to leave it until this morning. Not a bright idea as it turns out," he admitted with a grimace and then shook his head and said, "Ah well, I'll get by. At least there's a fireplace and plenty of chopped wood. I won't freeze."

The blonde's gaze shifted from his face to the road behind him and then she managed a smile, though he could still see the worry under the expression. "Well I have food stuff. You're welcome to it."

Teddy raised his eyebrows. "I thought you had provisions coming in today?"

She glanced away, briefly, but when she turned back, the cheerful smile had returned. "Yes, of course. I have loads of dry and canned goods, but someone was to deliver fruits and vegetables and stuff today. As well as gas for the generator."

"You have a generator?" Teddy asked with interest.

She nodded and then grimaced. "It's dead at the moment, though. They warned me there wasn't much gas in it but assured me more would be delivered today. I guess the generator must have kicked on when the power went off last night, but it died a few minutes ago. It's why I came out here. To watch for the delivery." She glanced along the road. "But I'm guessing the delivery guy isn't getting through anytime soon."

"No," Teddy agreed with a frown of his own, wondering how long her cottage would stay warm without the generator running. Probably not long, he decided and was about to offer to share his fire when she turned back to him and smiled wryly.

"So I have food and no heat and you have heat and no food. Care to share?"

Teddy sensed the worry under her smile and wondered about it, but then realized the poor girl was pretty much stranded alone in the woods in the middle of nowhere with a complete stranger. She didn't know him from Adam. Any woman would be worried. He could be an axe murderer, for all she knew.

"That sounds a sensible idea, young lady. But I guess I'd best introduce myself properly then." He held out one gloved hand. "My name is Theodore Brunswick. I'm police chief of a small town called Port Henry down south."

She stared blankly for a moment and then her lips widened. "That's so sweet."

Teddy blinked in confusion, not sure what the hell was sweet about his being police chief of Port Henry. It was a small town, but—

"You're trying to reassure me I'm safe with you," she explained. "That's really very sweet. Thank you."

"Oh." Teddy felt his face burning and knew it wasn't the cold air. He was blushing like a schoolboy, he realized with disgust and hoped to hell she put down any redness in his face to the cold. Retrieving his hand, he muttered, "Well, young women can't be too careful when they're on their own nowadays and I didn't want you worrying that I might be dangerous."

"You're right, of course," she said solemnly, and then pointed out cheerfully, "Of course, a rapist or serial killer would hardly introduce himself as one. In fact, claiming to be a cop would probably be the one thing most likely to lull a gal into feeling safe and give the creep an advantage."

Teddy's eyes widened and he turned fretfully to glance toward his cottage, saying, "I have my badge in the cottage. I can show it to you and my gun and—" He paused and glanced back as she began to chuckle.

"It's all right, I believe you," she assured him with a grin. "Why don't you go get that fire started while I fetch us some food from my cottage?"

"Sounds like a plan," Teddy muttered, feeling a bit off balance. There was just something about the girl . . . He watched her start away, envying the seeming ease with which she moved through the snow.

"Theodore?"

He raised his eyes to her face as she glanced back over her shoulder, noting the twinkle in her eyes and the naughty tilt to her grin. His voice was gruff as he said, "Call me Teddy."

"Teddy," she murmured as if tasting the word. Apparently, she liked it, because her smile widened, the naughtiness he'd noted now seeming to bloom until it completely took over her expression as her eyes drifted down over his figure to the groin of his jeans. She drawled, "I think I'd really like to see that gun of yours later."

Teddy felt his jaw drop, and gaped after her when she turned and continued away. Had she just— Surely she hadn't meant what he thought she—

"No," Teddy muttered, shaking his head. She hadn't meant what he thought. He was an old man, for Christ's sake, and she was a pretty young thing: young enough to be his granddaughter. Of course, she might not realize that yet. He was all bundled up against the cold, with little but his eyes and nose showing.

Teddy turned and started up his own driveway, reassuring himself that she wouldn't be interested once she got a look at his old mug. In fact, the poor girl would probably be embarrassed then, he thought with a wry chuckle. He was halfway back to the cottage before he realized she'd never told him her name.

Katricia whistled happily as she grabbed dried and canned food and packed it in the two empty boxes she'd found in a corner of the pantry. She wasn't really paying attention to what she was choosing, but then she had no idea what Teddy Brunswick would like—or what she herself would like, for that matter. It had been centuries since she'd bothered with mortal food.

"Katricia Argeneau Brunswick." It had a nice ring to it, she decided with a smile.

"Katricia and Teddy Argeneau Brunswick." Even better, she thought and sighed dreamily as she packed another can in the box.

Damn. She'd met her life mate. Katricia savored the thought. There was nothing in the world more important to an immortal than a life mate. It was what every one of them wanted and waited for, sometimes for centuries, sometimes even longer. Some never found one at all. But if they did, it was the most important moment in their life, finding that one person in the world, mortal or immortal, whom they couldn't read or control and with whom they could share their long life. It wasn't what Katricia had expected when she'd driven up here yesterday from Toronto. Though she probably should have, she acknowledged. Marguerite's matchmaking skills were becoming renowned. At least they were in the family. It was said she seemed to have the same ability that Katricia's grandmother and the family matriarch, Alexandria Argeneau, had possessed. That woman had found life mates for a good number of her children and the others of their kind before her death more than two thousand years ago. They said it had been like a sixth sense with her. Every couple she'd put together had been life mates. Now Marguerite was doing the same.

Still, this was the last thing Katricia had expected when Marguerite had invited her to join the family for Christmas. Especially since she'd said thank you, but no. It had been an automatic response. If she'd thought first, Katricia probably would have said yes, in the hopes that Marguerite had a life mate for her. However, she hadn't thought. Her answer had been automatic and firm. She avoided family gatherings. Actually, she avoided gatherings altogether. It was just too wearying to have to guard your thoughts all the time, so she'd taken to spending more and more time alone, especially the holidays, when all the older relatives got together. It was impossible to guard your thoughts from some of them, and Katricia didn't want one of her uncles reading hers.

The only family function she'd attended in the last decade was the multiple wedding in New York last February. Not showing up would have raised questions, since she lived and worked in New York, but as she'd expected, it had been hell. Concentrating on trying to guard her thoughts while trying to hold conversations with people had been like juggling knives while doing backflips. Impossible. She was sure more than one relative had caught a glimpse of her thoughts. She'd seen a flash of concern in the eyes of a couple of her uncles and even in Marguerite herself as she'd talked with her. Katricia was positive they all had caught how dark and depressing her thoughts were growing.

The thought made her smile. Both the darkness and depression had blown away like smoke in a stiff breeze the minute she'd reached the end of the driveway, spotted Teddy Brunswick, automatically tried to read his thoughts to see who he was and what he was doing there on the road, and found she couldn't. That had been a shocker. And suddenly her last-minute problems with her holiday plans had taken on a different light.

Katricia had been annoyed as hell when her flight from New York to Colorado for some holiday skiing had been diverted to Toronto. The pilot hadn't known what the problem was and Katricia had disembarked from the Argeneau plane ready to rip someone a new one, only to find her uncle, Lucian Argeneau, waiting on the tarmac.

"Bad weather," he'd announced by way of explanation as he'd bundled her into an SUV.

Katricia had been beside herself with frustration, her concentration divided between reciting nursery rhymes, to keep her uncle from reading her thoughts, and the intrusive worry that she'd be stuck with the family for the holidays and reciting those nursery rhymes for days. So, when he'd taken her to Marguerite's and that dear woman had mentioned that Decker had a cottage up north if she didn't wish to spend Christmas with the family, Katricia had jumped at the suggestion like a drowning woman leaping for a life raft. The next thing she'd known she and her luggage had been bundled in an SUV with the directions already on the GPS and she'd been on her way.

Now, here she was, up in the wilds of Central Ontario, snowed in with Teddy Brunswick, whom she couldn't read. Not being able to read a mortal was the first sign of a life mate. As an immortal, she could read mortals as easily as cracking open a book. Not being able to read Teddy had come as a hell of a shock. But a good one. A life mate. Damn, the idea made her sigh happily.

Of course, not being able to read him was only one of the signs, she tried to caution herself. After all, there was the occasional mortal that couldn't be read by anyone. They were usually crazies or people suffering from some affliction or other, like a brain tumor. Then no one could read them. However, Teddy Brunswick didn't seem mentally ill. He could still have a tumor or something, though, she acknowledged unhappily.

She would know soon enough, however. If Teddy really was her life mate, other symptoms would be showing up soon. The reawakening of her appetite for food was one of them, and she glanced curiously at the next box she lifted out and read the label.

"Bisquick."

She shrugged and stuck it in the box, but some of her good cheer was fading as she considered the one problem she could see with this scenario.

Katricia was pretty sure that bad weather hadn't been the reason for her diverted flight to ski country. She was absolutely certain that this had all been some grand plan to put her together with a possible life mate, which was all well and fine. But the snowstorm last night obviously hadn't been part of the plan and could be a problem, she thought with a frown.

Both boxes were now full of food. Katricia set one on top of the other, picked both up, and moved out of the pantry.

While she suspected Marguerite had arranged this meeting, she had no idea if Teddy knew about immortals. Most would probably call them vampires, but it was a term her people didn't care for. They were not cursed, soulless monsters, chomping on the neck of every passing mortal. While they lived long lives and didn't age beyond twenty-five or thirty, their physiology and need for blood was scientific in basis . . . and they avoided feeding on mortals now that blood banks were around. But just because she suspected Marguerite had sent her up here to find Teddy, it didn't mean he knew about their kind. Which meant she couldn't risk telling him the truth . . . that the provisions she'd been expecting weren't gas and food but gas and bagged blood. She didn't think he'd take well to learning he was snowed in with a vampire who was lacking in blood supplies right now.

Two

It didn't take Teddy long to get the fire going. He'd built it up to a roaring blaze in the hopes of warming the house faster, and had just straightened to head next door and help the girl with carting provisions over when he heard someone mounting the stairs to the deck. Hurrying to the door, he pulled it open and frowned as he stepped out into the vestibule to see his neighbor on the deck, trying to rearrange the boxes she carried to free a hand to knock.

"I was just coming to see if I could help. You shouldn't have carried all that by yourself," he admonished, quickly opening the door and reaching for one of the boxes.

"They aren't heavy," she assured him with a laugh, twisting and sliding past before he could take one.

Moving behind him, she set the boxes on the floor inside the open kitchen door and then sat on the bench across the end of the vestibule and set to work on removing her boots.

Teddy let the screen door close, and then firmly closed the wooden door against the chill before turning toward her. A frown crested his lips as she removed one boot and started on the other. They were covered with snow and couldn't be worn in the cottage, of course. It was why he'd removed his own on entering. But he still wore his coat, scarf, hat, and gloves. While the cottage was as cold as a walk-in refrigerator, the floor was like a slab of ice, and he could see her socks were your garden-variety everyday type, not meant for cold weather or icy cottages.

"Here." He slid his feet out of his slippers and pushed them toward her. "They'll be too big, but will keep you warm at least."

She glanced up with surprise. "What about you?"

"I have two pairs of thermal socks on. I'll be fine," he muttered, stepping into the kitchen and bending to pick up the boxes. Teddy grunted as he lifted them, surprised at how heavy they were. If the damned kid thought these weren't heavy, she must be a weight lifter or something, he thought with irritation as he hefted them onto the counter and then set them side by side to get a look at what they held.

"Thank you."

He glanced around as the blonde stepped into the cottage. She was shuffling her feet to keep the over-large slippers on, and it made a smile tug at his lips, but he forced it away. In his experience, young people embarrassed easily and he didn't want her to be uncomfortable. Glancing back to the boxes as she closed the kitchen door to the mudroom, he said, "You're welcome. What's your name?"

"Oh, I didn't introduce myself, did I?" she realized with a chuckle. Moving to join him at the counter, she began to remove items from the second box and said, "Katricia, but you can call me Tricia for short."

He noticed she hadn't mentioned a last name, but let it go for now and merely asked, "Why Tricia, and not Kat?" as he lifted out a can and examined the label to find it was tomato soup.

"Well, I always thought Kat sounded kind of bitchy," she answered absently as she worked. "Besides, men tend to like to play with that name, adding cutesy things like Kitty to it, or switching it out altogether for Kitty or even Pussy."

Teddy dropped the latest can he'd pulled out of the box and turned to her with amazement. "Pussy?"

She grinned at his expression and nodded. "Usually guys trying to get into my pants. Can you imagine a guy thinking that would tempt me to sleep with him?"

"Er." Teddy stared at her blankly, completely at a loss. Women just generally didn't talk quite so openly with him. They were usually kind of deferring and respectful. It was his title, of course. Being police chief meant people treated him differently. Well, most people anyway, he thought as Mabel and Elvi came to mind. Those two still treated him like the friend he'd been to them since their school years. Still, even they didn't say things like—

"You wouldn't think calling me Pussy Kat or even just Pussy would make me want to sleep with you, would you Teddy?"

He blinked as those husky words sank through his thoughts and realized that Katricia had turned her body to face his and moved closer. She was also looking up at him with soft blue eyes and slightly parted lips that made him think of Mary Martin back home. A year or two younger than he, and widowed, the woman was always on him like a tic on a deer whenever he entered a room. Mary had marriage on the mind and he didn't doubt it for a minute, but Teddy was too damned old to even consider marriage. He'd missed that boat, and while he regretted it, he—

His thoughts scattered as Katricia's pink little tongue slid out to run over her lips, wetting them. She had also continued to move closer, he realized with sudden alarm as her coat front brushed his and she raised a hand to brace it against his chest. His alarm only increased when he realized that he was swaying toward her in response like a moth drawn to a flame . . . a very old moth to a very young flame.

Giving his head a shake, Teddy quickly stepped back and began to remove his hat. It was still cold in the cottage, but it was time this little girl saw just who she was dealing with here. It would probably embarrass her to realize she'd been flirting with such an old fart, but it would be a damned sight more embarrassing for both of them if she didn't stop.

Avoiding looking at her so he didn't have to witness her horror as his gray hair was revealed, he moved across the room to set his hat on the dining-room table. Teddy then gave her another moment to deal with what he suspected would be her mortification at flirting with an old man by taking the time to remove his scarf, fold it neatly, and set it down before turning to reveal his weathered face.

He expected to find her wide-eyed and openmouthed with embarrassment. Instead, she eyed him with interest, as if inspecting a horse she was considering buying, and then she smiled and announced, "You're a good-looking man, Teddy Brunswick."

He blinked at the words and frowned. "I'm an *old* man."

The words made her chuckle, and she shook her head. "You're not twenty-five, but that doesn't mean you aren't good-looking. You have a strong face, nice eyes, and a full head of sexy, silver hair." When he just frowned harder, she added, "What? You thought your age made you unattractive? How many women do you think would say no to Sean Connery?"

The question made his eyes widen, and Katricia grinned. She also removed her own hat and scarf. Much to his relief, she didn't come near him but set them neatly on the counter beside her and then turned back to the box of goods to continue emptying it.

The moment she did, Teddy felt some of the stress slip from his body. But he didn't move back to join her; instead, he eyed her from where he stood, taking in her profile. She wasn't a beauty. Her hair was blond, whereas he had always preferred redheads, and her face was pale, her features more fitting in a Renaissance portrait, but there was something appealing about her, he decided and then quickly tried to erase that thought from his mind.

There was nothing at all appealing about this young woman, he lectured himself firmly. She was a child. Barely twenty-five, by his guess. A baby, compared to him. And he wasn't going to forget that. Teddy Brunswick was not going to be one of those old fools chasing around little girls young enough to be his granddaughter. Nope, he wasn't going to be the kind of man others snickered about behind his back.

Suitably chastened, Teddy moved to the fire and threw another log on, then took a minute to push the logs around until the fire was full-strength. Satisfied by the heat pouring off of it, he glanced around the room and then toward the hall to the bedrooms. He could see the open bedroom doors and frowned.

"What's wrong?" Katricia asked and he glanced over to see that she'd stopped unpacking and was watching him curiously.

"I was just thinking I should close the bedroom doors so the heat stays in here," he admitted, setting the poker back on its holder.

"I'll do it," she offered and moved off at once.

Teddy let her go, thinking she would find the bathroom that way so she didn't have to ask when she needed to use it. With her safely out of the room, he moved back to the boxes to continue sorting the contents. He almost sighed aloud when he found the can of coffee. Of course, the coffee pot wouldn't work without electricity, but maybe if he boiled some water in a pot over the fire and then used the drip filter and coffee pot, he could come up with a halfway decent brew. A cup of coffee sounded damned fine at that moment. It might help clear his thoughts some, too, he decided and set the can aside to start searching the cupboards for a suitable pot.

Katricia took her time closing bedroom doors, peering curiously into each room as she went. It was partially out of curiosity and partially to give Teddy some breathing room. She didn't need to read his mind to know that he wasn't comfortable with her. She supposed she'd come on too strong too fast, but hadn't been able to help herself. The very fact that he might be her life mate made her want to test it. She wasn't hungry yet, but then the only food around was in cans and boxes. There was nothing really to tempt her palate. Which meant the easiest way to know for sure was to kiss Teddy and see if she experienced the shared pleasure she'd heard so much about.

Unfortunately, it was looking like that might be a hard objective to achieve. Teddy didn't appear to be comfortable with what he thought was their age difference. That seemed obvious to her from the way he'd quickly removed his hat and scarf and then turned as if presenting some monstrosity to her. This was going to take some patience, which had never been Katricia's strong suit. She was already struggling with the urge to simply walk straight back out into the kitchen and jump the man's bones. The only thing stopping her was the worry that she might give the poor guy a heart attack or something.

That would be just her luck—kill her life mate with a heart attack before she could woo and turn him.

Grimacing at the thought, Katricia continued checking out the rooms. She found the one with Teddy's suitcase in it and smiled faintly, thinking it was the room she would have picked, too. It was the last on the left, with the window overlooking the driveway where he could easily look out to see who was approaching should anyone come up the drive.

It was a good defensive position, and his cop was showing in the choice, she thought with a smile and then pulled the door closed and moved back up the hall. Her eyes widened slightly when she found Teddy kneeling by the fireplace, situating a couple of pots at the edge of the fire.

"What are you doing?" she asked curiously, moving up behind him to peer over his shoulder, but moving back a bit when she sensed him stiffening.

"Experimenting," he said gruffly, straightening and moving around her to get back into the kitchen. "Boiling water to make drip coffee and heating chicken soup. It's not the usual breakfast fare, I know, but beggars can't be choosers."

"Clever," Katricia murmured, watching from the fireplace as he moved into the kitchen and began to measure coffee into a filter.

"Hardly clever," Teddy said with amusement as he set his coffee fixings aside and continued rifling through the box. "More like desperate. I'm useless without my java."

"Java?" Katricia asked, warming her hands at the fire.

"Coffee," he explained and then said, "Since you're over there, keep an eye on the soup for me, will you?"

"Sure," Katricia said, watching him cross to the table to redon his hat and scarf.

"I'm going to go see if I can get my truck door open and the truck started so I can charge my phone," he explained as he moved to the door. "If I can get the phone hooked up, I can call Marguerite and see if we can't get the power back on."

"Marguerite?"

Teddy paused to glance her way with surprise. Probably because she'd barked the word in her surprise, she thought and grimaced to herself. Clearing her throat, she asked more calmly, "Who's Marguerite?"

"Marguerite Argeneau, a friend. She arranged for me to rent this cottage. I want to call and find out who I should report the power problem to," he said slowly, still eyeing her a little oddly. But then he shook his head and turned to walk out into the mudroom to don his boots. He pulled the door closed behind him and Katricia stared at it, biting her lip.

She had a cell phone. It was in her pocket and had been since waking and yet she hadn't once thought of using it . . . not even to check on her blood delivery. That more than anything told her just how overset she'd been since finding she couldn't read Teddy.

Muttering under her breath, she pulled out the phone, but then paused and simply stood there, listening until Teddy finished donning his boots and she heard him stomp out of the cottage.

Katricia then turned to give the soup a quick stir before moving into the kitchen to peer out the window. Spotting Teddy by the door of his pickup, fiddling with the lock, she quickly pulled up contacts on her phone and found her aunt's listing. Marguerite answered on the second ring, her voice cheerful and happy as she said, "Hello Tricia, dear, how is your vacation going?"

"I can't read Teddy," Katricia blurted, not bothering with niceties.

"Oh, how lovely!" Marguerite didn't sound at all surprised. "I hoped the two of you would meet. Isn't he a handsome man?"

"Yes," Katricia breathed. Teddy Brunswick was the most beautiful man she'd ever met. Of course she might be biased, since she couldn't read him and suspected he was her life mate. It tended to color things. Still, he *was* a handsome man.

"He's so dignified-looking, and such a gentleman. I've seen pictures of him when he was younger and I promise you he'll be even more gorgeous after he's turned. He——"

"Does he know about us?" Katricia interrupted, zeroing in on what was most important to her. If he knew about them, she could just tell him she couldn't read him and then jump his bones and find out for sure whether he was her life mate or not.

"Yes, he does, dear. He's the police chief in Port Henry, a nice little town where your uncle Victor now lives with his Elvi. Many people know about us there. You can let him know what you are. He won't be horrified."

"How much does he know exactly?" Katricia asked. "I mean, does he know about life mates and such?"

Marguerite hesitated briefly, and Katricia was sure she was about to say no, but instead, her aunt said, "Well . . . yes, he does know about that, dear. However, it might be a good idea if you don't blurt out that you can't read him until he's gotten a chance to get to know you a little better."

"What?" Katricia asked with alarm and then almost whined, "But why?"

Marguerite chuckled softly. "I know it's tempting to just tell him that he's your life mate and so on right away, but——"

"Is he?" Katricia interrupted eagerly.

"Is he what? Your life mate?" Marguerite asked with surprise. "I thought you said you couldn't read him?"

"Well, I can't, but sometimes mortals can't be read because—"

"Teddy is very readable," Marguerite interrupted soothingly. "In fact, you're the first immortal I have heard of who can't read him. Even Elvi and Mabel are beginning to be able to read him and they're still quite new to this business."

"Oh," Katricia breathed and bit her lip. "But then why shouldn't I tell him—"

"He's mortal, dear," Marguerite interrupted gently. "It might be a little much for him to handle so soon. Just let him get to know you a little better first, maybe. You don't want him jumping in his truck and heading back to Port Henry in a panic."

"He can't," Katricia assured her and then quickly explained about the tree blocking the road and the power outage.

"Oh dear," Marguerite breathed when she finished. "I'll call Lucian and have him send some men to clear the road and—"

"Oh, no, don't do that," Katricia said at once. "If the road's cleared he might leave. Besides, right now I'm staying at his cottage and sharing Decker's food with him. If you clear the road—"

"There won't be any need for you to both be at his cottage," Marguerite finished for her with understanding and then paused briefly before asking, "So you have heat and food?"

"Yes."

"I suppose there's no real urgency to clear the road and get the power back on, then," Marguerite murmured. "But call at once if the situation changes and you need things fixed quickly."

"I will."

"I'll call Bastien about the blood delivery though," Marguerite went on. "They can bring it in by snowmobile. Perhaps they can even arrange for a snowmobile to be brought for the two of you to use. That way you can still share the cottage but also get out to get provisions if you need them, or even just get out for a meal so you don't get cabin fever."

"That would be nice," Katricia said, a smile curving her lips as she imagined Teddy sitting behind her on a snowmobile, his arms wrapped around her as they roared off into town for groceries or dinner. Or even herself on the back, holding on to him as he drove them back. In her experience, men tended to prefer to drive and she was willing to share . . . especially if it meant getting to ride with her arms around him and her chest pressed to his back and—

Dear God, I'm pathetic, Katricia thought with a shake of the head. "Are you sure I can't just tell him? He might be all right with it if he knew."

"He might," Marguerite agreed uncertainly. "I just think it's better to err on the side of caution. This life-mate business is such a delicate thing. I'm just suggesting you maybe wait a day or two. Right now you're a stranger to him, dear."

"Yeah," Katricia agreed on a sigh, her gaze moving to Teddy out by the truck.

"I'll suggest Bastien have the blood courier bring food, too," Marguerite said suddenly. "And more blankets and— It might take a while to get everything together, Katricia. Are you okay for blood if it doesn't show until tomorrow morning or later?"

"Yeah, I'm good," Katricia assured her. "I can go two or three days without if I have to. Twenty-four hours is nothing."

"All right then, leave it to me. I'll take care of everything."

Three

Teddy gave up on the lock with an irritated curse.
He wasn't getting into the vehicle any time soon
unless he wanted to break one of the windows, and he
wasn't ready to do that. He might have, if the situation
had been a desperate one, but it wasn't. They had heat,
food, and shelter. They even had coffee. They could
stick it out for a bit.

Sighing, he stepped back from the truck and
glanced up toward the road, debating walking up to
see if there was any sign of the snow removal men, or
if a work crew had arrived to tend to the fallen trees.
In the end, he decided against it. It really wasn't very
likely. While Marguerite had said the county cleared
the road, Teddy suspected this just wasn't likely to be
a high-priority street. In fact, it was probably one of

the last ones tended to. Which meant it would probably be late today or maybe even tomorrow morning
before the road crew would make it out here to clear the
road and see the downed power lines. And that meant
it would probably be tomorrow or even the day after
before someone came to take care of the power problem. But since the day after tomorrow was Christmas
Day, it wasn't likely to get taken care of then, either.
They could be stuck here until Boxing Day without
power. That meant chicken soup, or even tomato soup
for Christmas dinner, he thought with a grimace.

"Merry Christmas," he muttered to himself, turning
to walk back toward the deck. He was mounting the
stairs before it occurred to him that the water might
be boiling by now. He could make an attempt at coffee,
Teddy realized. The possibility cheered him and made
him move more swiftly.

The cottage was noticeably warmer when he finished removing his boots in the mudroom and stepped
inside. It was even warm enough that Teddy thought
he could remove his coat this time along with his hat
and scarf. He started to do so but paused when he
saw that Katricia had already removed her own . . . as
well as the bottoms to her ski suit, he noted as his gaze
landed on her where she stood bent over in front of
the fireplace, stirring the soup. She was now wearing

a baby-blue sweater and a pair of what almost looked like leotards the pants were so thin and molded to her skin. She may as well have been nude, but as tightly as the cloth hugged her, there wasn't a panty line to be seen. She couldn't be wearing anything under them, he realized, his eyes moving over the curves with fascination. Honest to God, he wouldn't have been surprised to hear that she wasn't wearing anything at all and that her skin was just airbrushed the dark blue of the leotards. Damn, she had the shapeliest little ass and legs he'd seen in a long time.

"The water's boiling, but I wasn't sure if I should pour it in that thing you set up or wait for you to come back in first. Should I do it now?"

Teddy blinked at the question and forced his gaze away from Katricia's tight bottom as she glanced over her shoulder toward him.

"Er . . . no, that's okay, I'll do it," he muttered, forcing himself to finish removing his jacket. He stuffed his hat and scarf in the pockets and then hung it on the back of one of the chairs at the dining-room table, noting she'd done the same with her ski jacket and pants. It was better than hanging them back up in the mudroom where they'd be unpleasantly cold to don. Speaking of which, he decided he should find a towel, set it on the kitchen floor by the door, and bring their boots in to thaw. It would be nice not to put his feet in stiff, snow-encrusted boots the next time he went out.

Deciding he'd better do it while he was thinking of it, Teddy nipped quickly into his room to dig out the large bath towel he'd packed. He folded it twice as he carried it back out, then set it on the floor and retrieved both his boots and Katricia's from the mudroom to set them on it.

Aware that the soup was probably boiling, too, Teddy then grabbed both oven mitts off the top of the micro-wave and moved over to the fire. Katricia straightened and moved aside as he approached, giving him space, and he felt relief slide through him. It seemed he'd been right and now that she saw how old he was, she was going to cut out that silly flirtatious nonsense.

"How long has the soup been boiling?" he asked as he slid the gloves on.

"Several minutes now," Katricia answered and then, sounding a little awed, murmured, "It smells lovely."

Teddy glanced at her with surprise. It was just tinned soup, nothing to write home about, he thought, but then smiled wryly, knowing that—like himself—she probably hadn't eaten since yesterday. Truth to tell, tinned soup or not, he was hungry enough that it was smelling good to him, too, he acknowledged as he lifted both pots away from the fire.

Katricia followed when he carried them carefully over to the kitchen area, but stayed to hover over the soup pan when he set it on the stove to cool. Leaving her there, he moved over to slowly pour the water into the filter cone he'd removed from the coffee machine and set on top of the coffee pot.

A little sigh of anticipation slid from his lips as steam rose to mist his face with the aroma of brewing coffee. Teddy had to restrain himself from simply dumping the liquid impatiently into the cone, but anything worth doing was worth doing right. Besides, he wanted good coffee, not muck. He glanced at Katricia. She was leaning over the soup, eyes closed and inhaling the steam rising from it, and it made him smile slightly.

"Why don't you fetch a couple bowls and a ladle and serve it up," he suggested.

Katricia didn't have to be prompted twice; she was immediately slipping around him to get to the items he'd suggested. By the time he poured the last of the water into the cone, she'd divided the soup between two bowls, found soup spoons for both of them, and then picked them up, but paused to ask, "Do you want to eat at the table or by the fire?"

"By the fire," Teddy decided as he fetched coffee cups for both of them. While it was warmer in the cottage than it had been, and it had seemed pleasant when he'd first come in from the cold, now that he'd been inside a few minutes, he was aware that it was chillier the farther you got away from the fire.

Leaving Katricia to carry the soup into the living room, Teddy quickly poured them each a coffee, then grabbed spoons, the sugar bowl, and some powdered creamer from the cupboard and followed her. When she pushed the coffee table a little closer to the fire and sat on the carpet on one side of it, he moved around to the other side and set down their coffees and fixings.

"Mmmm."

Teddy glanced up from fixing his coffee to see that Katricia had neglected the chore to dive right into her soup. He smiled with amusement as she sighed with pleasure at the simple fare. "I'm guessing your mother isn't much of a cook."

She looked surprised at the suggestion. "Why would you say that?"

"Because if you think a heated-up tin of salty soup with limp noodles in it is moan-worthy, you haven't had good cooking, little girl," he assured her.

"Hmm." She tilted her head and then said, "Well, first of all, I'm not a little girl, and second, no one cooks for me. I don't live with my mother and haven't done so for a very, very long time."

"Hell, two weeks is a very very long time to kids your age," he said with a laugh and then asked, "So where do you live?"

"New York."

Teddy blinked at the answer. He'd expected her to say at university or some such thing. New York was an entirely different kettle of fish: the big city, crime central. He wouldn't have let his daughter live there, had he had one. Sitting back, he eyed her more closely. She was athletic in build, with shoulders a little wider than her hips, and a smaller bosom. Teddy generally preferred curvy women. At least, Elvi, the woman he'd loved most of his life, was curvy. Elvi was also a red-head whereas this girl was a fresh-faced blonde, and yet he found her strangely appealing.

Reining in his thoughts, Teddy frowned and turned his gaze down to his soup as he asked, "What do you do there?"

"I'm presently in law enforcement, but I'm considering alternate career choices at the moment."

Teddy glanced up sharply at this announcement, but she was now peering into her own soup and scooping out a spoonful.

"Law enforcement?" he asked with a surprise that was close to horror. "In New York?"

The thought of this little gal chasing after criminals in the Big Apple was a staggering one. Hell, he wouldn't want to do it himself, and he'd been in law enforcement most of his life and the army before that. Still, with a choice between a war zone or New York, he'd take the war zone. "I'm not surprised you're considering a career change so soon."

She glanced up, smiling faintly at his expression, and said, "It's not soon . . . I've been in law enforcement for almost a century."

Teddy froze, a spoonful of soup halfway to his mouth. He lifted narrowed eyes to her face, focusing on it firmly for the first time since meeting her. Before this, he hadn't wanted to make her uncomfortable by staring too hard, but now he did, focusing specifically on her eyes and noting the silver glimmering among the blue. Setting his spoon back in his bowl, he said quietly, "Immortal."

Tricia nodded solemnly. "My name is Katricia Argeneau. Marguerite is my aunt by marriage."

Teddy just stared at her, having to readjust every thought in his woolly mind. He'd been thinking of her as a poor, defenseless, young gal snowed in out here in the wilds. Instead, she was an immortal, nowhere near defenseless . . . or young, for that matter, he realized. At least, not if she'd been in law enforcement for almost a century. Which changed everything, of course. His gaze slid down over her upper body in her baby-blue sweater. She looked young, but she wasn't, so he hadn't been lusting after a sweet young thing. Not that he'd been lusting after her, Teddy assured himself quickly, but found himself suddenly fighting the urge to ask if she wanted to see his "gun" now.

Giving his head a shake, he cleared his throat and asked, "By law enforcement, I suppose you mean you're one of those council enforcers? A rogue hunter who works under Lucian?"

She nodded, watching him closely.

Teddy's eyes slid to the soup she'd been gobbling up, and he frowned. Most immortals didn't eat after the first century or two, so she couldn't be over two hundred. Eyes narrowing, he tilted his head to consider her solemnly. "The provisions you were expecting? Not just gas and food?"

"Blood, too," she admitted quietly.

"Do you have any at all with you?"

Katricia shook her head. "I had a couple bags in the SUV with me, but drank them before retiring after I arrived."

Teddy pursed his lips at this news and then gestured to her soup. "But you still eat."

She hesitated, but then simply nodded.

He sat back with a sigh and considered this new wrinkle in the situation. He was snowed in, had scanty provisions and no power, and his companion was a vampire with no blood supplies . . . except him. "So you're telling me this now because . . . what? You need a blood donor?"

"No," she said with a laugh. "I'm good for now and the blood delivery will show before I need a 'blood donor,' as you put it."

"Not with the road the way it is," he pointed out dryly.

Katricia shrugged, not seeming concerned, and he understood why when she said, "They'll bring it by snowmobile if they can't get through on the road. They won't leave me without."

Teddy felt himself relax a little at that news, relieved to be off the menu, but then asked, "So why are you telling me now? How did you know I knew about your kind?"

"Aunt Marguerite," she answered simply. "You mentioned her name and then I recalled that the immortal-friendly town my uncle Victor lives in is called Port Henry." She shrugged. "Since you knew Aunt Marguerite, I figured you knew."

Teddy didn't respond at first. He could usually spot a lie a mile off, and Ms. Argeneau was lying . . . about something. The problem was he wasn't sure what she was lying about exactly. What she said seemed reasonable enough, but he had to wonder why she hadn't admitted all of this when he'd first mentioned Marguerite.

"Of course, if you hadn't known, your reaction to my claiming to be in enforcement for a century would have told me and I would have acted like I was joking or something," she added in a rush as she reached for her coffee.

Teddy narrowed his eyes further as he watched her sip from her mug. The way she was avoiding his eyes and the sudden rush of words just confirmed it in his mind that she was lying. He was about to call her on it, when she wrinkled her nose over the taste of the coffee and set it back with a grimace.

"Ugh. You can't start your day without this stuff?"

"It tastes better with cream and sugar," he said absently, pushing them both toward her. He was about to ask what exactly she was lying about and why, when he suddenly knew the answer. After his mentioning her aunt, Katricia had probably read his thoughts and learned he knew about their kind. She was lying to keep him from being uncomfortable with her reading his mind.

"Oh, yes, this is much better."

Teddy glanced to her to find that she'd doctored her coffee with the sugar and creamer and tried it again . . . and apparently enjoyed it this way. She was actually gulping it down eagerly now.

"I'd go slow if I were you," he cautioned with amusement. "Some immortals can't handle caffeine."

"They can't?" she asked with surprise.

Teddy shook his head. "Victor does all right on it, and DJ can handle a cup or two, but Alessandro is wired when he drinks it. Starts going ninety like he's on some kind of vampire speed or crack, and then passes out."

"I know DJ is Uncle Victor's friend, but who is Alessandro?" Katricia asked curiously before downing the rest of her drink.

"Alessandro Cipriano," Teddy explained. "He's another immortal who lives in Port Henry."

"Ah." She nodded, but had twisted to peer toward the coffee pot on the counter. In the next instant, she was on her feet and snatching up both their cups.

Teddy just shook his head and continued eating his soup, but his gaze was on her as she crossed the room to pour them both a fresh cup, specifically on her behind. The woman might be over a century old, but she had the body of a sweet young thing and the tightest little behind he'd ever seen. She definitely didn't have any panties on under those leotards of hers, he thought as he watched her butt cheeks shift with each step. If he peeled the leotards off, he was sure he'd find nothing but her pale, perfect flesh.

"Unless you're ready to show me your gun, you should really stop looking at me like that."

Teddy forced his eyes from Katricia's behind and up to find her peering at him over her shoulder. He flushed first at being caught staring so rudely at her butt, then reddened further as her words sank in. Damn, that definitely sounded like a proposition. The problem was he didn't have a damned clue how to respond to it, and suspected he'd stutter like a schoolboy if he tried. The women he knew just weren't so . . . er . . . forward . . . or comely, for that matter. Not that there weren't attractive women in Port Henry. He'd been attracted to plenty of women there, many of them his own age. But it had been a while . . . and there was just something about Katricia that— Well, basically, his gun was loaded and half-cocked just from looking at her . . . and wasn't that the saddest thing in the world? If he took her up on what he suspected was an offer, he'd probably empty his barrel before he even took aim . . . so to speak.

"My gun's in the drawer there if you want to see it," he said finally, turning his gaze to his soup as she started back across the room. "So is my badge."

She let him get away with pretending to misunderstand and simply set his coffee cup in front of him and settled on the floor across from him to fix her own. But the thought was in his head now, and he couldn't look at her without his mind running along rather X-rated lines, starting with peeling off those damned leotards and running his hands over the firm flesh beneath. His hands, his lips, his tongue . . . Hell, he'd never been a biter, but Teddy had a sudden urge to nip one of the round cheeks and see if it was as firm as it looked, and then—

A sudden ache between his legs brought Teddy's attention to the fact that he was no longer just half-cocked. He now sported a full-fledged erection that was pressing against his jeans, begging to be released. Christ. He was reacting like a twelve-year-old boy who just found his dad's stash of porn magazines . . . and the woman was fully clothed, for God's sake. How pathetic was that? Obviously, he needed to keep a tight rein on his eyes and his thoughts, Teddy decided grimly. In fact, since she was immortal and could read his thoughts if she wanted, he should have been doing it already. The realization made him glance warily to her expression. Katricia was smiling slightly, not looking offended. She hadn't read his mind, he decided with relief. Still, he determined not to even look at her again while he finished his soup and second cup of coffee.

The fire was dying down by the time they finished and carried their dishes to the kitchen sink. Teddy then returned to add several logs to the blaze and rearrange them in the flames for maximum benefit. He then considered the logs left in the dwindling stack beside the fireplace and moved to begin donning his coat and boots.

"Where are you going?" Katricia asked with surprise.

"To fetch more wood for the fire," he answered, doing up his boots.

"I'll help." She was immediately donning her own coat and boots.

"There's no need in both of us getting cold," he said quietly.

"Why not? The fire warms both of us," she said with a laugh and simply pulled on her gloves.

Teddy frowned, but let it go. He'd learned from dealing with Elvi and Mabel over the years that there was really just no use arguing with a strong woman. Most women would have been happy to leave him to it while they played little housemate inside, but Elvi and Mabel wouldn't have, and he suspected Katricia was made of the same velvet-covered steel that his two friends were. A woman didn't work in law enforcement, whether it was mortal or immortal, without a solid backbone.

"The air may be cold, but I don't think I've ever breathed anything so clean," Katricia said as they started off the porch.

Teddy smiled faintly. "I suppose there isn't a whole lot of clean air in New York."

"Too many cars for that," she said wryly.

"Do you like the city?" he asked curiously as they crossed the yard to the small shed with the tarp-covered wood stacked beside it.

"Not really," she said easily and laughed at his surprise. "I suppose you're now wondering why I stay there then?"

"You'd suppose right," he said mildly.

Katricia shrugged as they paused and pulled the tarp back to begin gathering wood. "It was exciting when I first settled there. The place to be. Life can get boring after a couple of centuries, but New York seemed alive, vibrant, with loads to do and see." She smiled wryly. "It's why most older immortals gravitate there, and a lot have settled there over the decades."

"Really?" he asked curiously, waiting as she shifted her load and tugged the tarp back into place.

Katricia nodded. "New York and Los Angeles are the most popular places for our kind in the States, and Toronto and Montreal hold the most immortals in Canada."

"The most populated cities," Teddy murmured as they started back toward the cottage.

Katricia nodded. "The more people there are, the later things stay open and the more things there are to do to entertain yourself . . . and, of course, back when we had to feed off the hoof, the more possible donors there were around to choose from."

Teddy grimaced at the reminder that immortals had at one time fed off his people. Now that there were blood banks, they were restricted only to bagged blood and had laws against biting mortals except in cases of emergency. Katricia had been alive long enough to have had to feed off the hoof at one time, he realized and glanced at her curiously, imagining her roaming the streets of New York in search of victims.

"Stop that," she said on a laugh.

"What?" he asked, forcing his gaze away as they mounted the stairs to the cottage.

"Stop looking at me like you expect my fangs to sprout and me to fall on your throat at any moment," she said dryly. "We don't do that anymore."

Teddy remained silent as they entered the cottage and shed their boots to carry the wood to the stack beside the fireplace, but once they'd laid down their burden, he asked, "So you moved to New York for the excitement, but don't enjoy it anymore?"

She shrugged and turned to walk back to their boots. "New York has its charms. I like the theater, and it has some great clubs, but there are just some things it doesn't have." She started to undo her coat, and then paused and asked, "Do you want to walk up to the road and see if the snow removers have arrived yet?"

"Sure," he agreed easily. It was better than sitting around inside, he supposed as he joined her to redon his boots. Once they were headed out of the cottage again, he asked, "So what are the things New York doesn't have?"

"Stars at night," she said at once. "I couldn't believe it when I got up here and saw all the stars in the sky. I'd forgotten there were so many."

Teddy nodded in understanding. The closer you were to a city the fewer stars there appeared to be in the sky. You saw a lot of stars in the sky down in Port Henry, but even there you didn't see as many as up here. They were too close to London, he supposed.

"And the fresh air," Katricia added solemnly. "Sometimes it feels like you're sucking on a muffler in New York."

Teddy chuckled at the image that put in his head.

"And the peace and quiet. I mean just listen." She suddenly paused, closed her eyes, and raised her head in a listening attitude, and Teddy did the same. Silence immediately surrounded him and then he became aware of his breathing, hers, the soft sounds of small creatures moving through the snowy woods, the soft thud of snow sliding off a branch or something else nearby and hitting the snow-covered ground. It was as close to absolute silence as a body could get, he acknowledged.

Katricia sighed almost blissfully. "No traffic, no hum of engines or factories, no chatter of people. Nothing. You can never find silence in New York."

Teddy opened his eyes and nodded solemnly. Even in Port Henry it was rare, though not impossible to find. They began to walk again, as if by agreement, and he asked, "So why don't you move?"

"I just might," she said lightly. "Are there any openings for law enforcement in Port Henry?"

Teddy chuckled at the question. "Actually, there will be soon."

"Really?" she asked with interest.

Teddy nodded. "I'll talk to Lucian and if he gives you a good recommendation, we'll see what we can do."

When she didn't respond, he glanced over to see that she was grinning. It seemed she didn't mind the idea of giving up New York for small-town life, but he cautioned, "Port Henry isn't nearly as exciting as New York. You have to travel half an hour to get to the nearest movie theater or play, and there isn't a single night club there."

"Sounds good to me," she said lightly.

Teddy smiled faintly and shook his head.

"So, have you always lived in Port Henry?" she asked.

"Born and bred," he said quietly, and then admitted, "Though I left for a bit to join the army."

"And how did you like that?" Katricia asked curiously.

"It had its good points and bad points I suppose," he said slowly. "They taught me discipline and how to handle myself. Made me a man, I guess. And I got to see a bit of the world, but I missed Port Henry."

"You sound surprised," she teased lightly.

"I sort of was," he admitted with a laugh. "All the time I was growing up in Port Henry my feet were itching to get me out of there, see the world, do things, go places." He chuckled at his younger self and shook his head. "I guess it took leaving to appreciate what I had in Port Henry."

"Isn't there an old saying, you don't know what you've got till it's gone?" she asked with amusement. "Or maybe it's song lyrics."

"Or both," he said quietly. "Whatever the case, it's true. Or it was for me."

She was silent for a minute and then asked, "Have you ever been married, Teddy?"

He shook his head. "Never had the pleasure. You?"

She chuckled wryly. "No. But then that's not unusual for my kind. We can go centuries or even millennia before finding our life mate."

"Ah yes, the immortal's life mate," Teddy said quietly. "That one person that an immortal can't read or control. The one they can relax and be themselves around."

"It's more than that," Katricia said solemnly. "Everything is better with a life mate. Food tastes better, colors are brighter, everything is just . . . more . . . and, of course, we can experience shared dreams and shared pleasure, which is supposed to be better than anything ever." She released a gusty little sigh. "I can't wait."

Teddy took in her happy smile and chuckled. "You need to talk to Marguerite, then. I hear she's like some kind of mystic matchmaker for your people, the queen of immortal hook-ups. She'll have you experiencing that shared pleasure in no time if you put yourself in her hands."

"Wouldn't you like to experience it too?"

Teddy glanced at her with surprise, and then reminded her, "I'm mortal. We don't have life mates."

"Mortals can be life mates to immortals," she pointed out with a shrug.

"Yeah." Teddy was silent, considering that. He'd seen it happen several times now, and in truth he was envious as hell over it. But he wasn't foolish enough to hold out much hope of something like that happening to him.

"Hmmm."

Teddy glanced around curiously at that mutter from Katricia to see that they'd not only reached the end of the driveway but had traversed the ten feet to the bend in the road . . . and it looked exactly as it had the first time he'd seen it. The trees still lay on the road, and the road itself was still snow-covered for as far as he could see. "Looks like we aren't likely to be getting out of here any time soon."

"Good thing we have food and firewood, then," Katricia said cheerfully, turning away to start back.

Teddy nodded, but didn't follow at once. Instead, he stood staring up the road, wondering how long it would take them to trudge up to the road if it wasn't cleared in the next day or so. They weren't likely to run out of firewood: there were several cords lined up along the shed, enough to last a hell of a long time. But the two boxes of food might not last all that long. Still, maybe they'd get lucky and the road crews would be along sometime today. And then maybe they'd get really lucky and the downed trees would be moved and the power lines fixed today or tomorrow. If so, they could head into town and buy groceries. He'd get a big turkey and all the fixings and they could cook up a fine Christmas dinner to share.

The idea made him smile, a nice, cozy Christmas dinner with Katricia. Maybe he'd buy her a gift, too. Something small, so she wouldn't feel bad for not having a gift for him, and he could get stockings and fill them with chocolate and some thermal socks for her, and—

Teddy's thoughts died as something smacked him in the back of the head and nearly startled him into falling on his butt. Managing to keep his feet under him, he turned in surprise and gaped at Katricia as she bent to scoop up more snow into her hands.

"You looked like you'd fallen asleep on your feet," she said with a grin. "I thought I'd wake you up."

"Wake me up, huh?" he asked, eyes narrowing on the snowball she was even now forming in her hands. Teddy stood completely still until she took aim and loosed the ball, then ducked and snatched up snow of his own as hers flew overhead. "You made a big mistake there, little lady. I am a champion at snowball fights."

"Yeah?" she asked with a laugh, scooping up more snow herself. "Bring it on."

Four

"Gin!" Katricia squealed gleefully as she set down her cards.

"Again?" Teddy squawked, throwing his own hand down with disgust. "You have to be cheating."

Katricia laughed at the accusation. "How could I have cheated? You dealt the hand."

"Hmm," Teddy muttered.

Katrina quickly added up their cards and marked down their new scores, then gathered the cards. As she began to shuffle, Teddy glanced at the fire and then leaned to the side to move the screen aside and toss on another log. Katricia watched him with a smile. After their snowball fight, which they'd decided had been a draw, they'd come in and warmed up by the fire with more lovely hot coffee before they'd heated up some sort of soup Teddy had called chunky something or other. Then they'd chatted and played cards through the afternoon, indulging in poker and rummy until dinnertime.

Another chunky-type soup had been dinner, but this time with some kind of dumplings made from the Bisquick that he'd cooked in it. Teddy had warned her the dumplings wouldn't be as good as they should be, since he'd only had powdered milk to work with, but they had tasted delicious to her. After doing their best to clean up after dinner, a task that was made difficult by the need to heat water over the fire to get it warm enough to clean with, they'd returned to playing cards and chatting again. This time though, Teddy had decided to teach her gin, which she was quite enjoying since it was the first game she was winning every hand. With the other games, it had been pretty even, one winning a hand, then the other. But she was absolutely trouncing him in gin . . . and doing so with glee.

"This game is fun," Katricia said cheerfully as she finished shuffling. "I can't believe I've never heard of it before."

"Neither can I," Teddy said dryly as he used the poker to shift the logs around to his satisfaction. "You play like a pro."

"Beginner's luck," she assured him with a grin he didn't catch. He was setting the poker back.

"Hmm." Teddy turned and began to pick up and arrange the cards in his hand.

"So," Katricia said as she finished dealing and set down the remaining cards. "What's this job you mentioned coming up in Port Henry?"

Teddy glanced at her with surprise. They hadn't talked about that since he'd mentioned it during their walk that morning, but she had been thinking about it. While she was growing weary of hunting rogues, Katricia thought she might enjoy working on the force in Port Henry, especially if it meant working closely with Teddy. She already knew they worked well together. They had functioned as a team when they'd set out to make lunch and then supper, and then while cleaning up afterward. It had been rather scary in a way, how in sync they'd been, she thought, as if they'd been doing it for centuries.

"Would you really be interested?" he asked curiously.

Katricia nodded.

Teddy hesitated, and then pointed out, "It wouldn't be nearly as exciting as hunting rogues."

Katricia smiled wryly at the words. Rogues were immortals who had broken one of their laws, usually older immortals who hadn't found a life mate and had grown weary of living. It was her theory that they were mostly looking for a way out. Suicide by enforcer, basically. She understood, in a way, at least the weariness. Katricia had experienced that herself the last century or so . . . until meeting Teddy. What she didn't understand was the need the rogue seemed to have to hurt others on the way down, usually mortals. They turned them in droves, or tortured them, or did whatever would catch the council's notice quickly and force them to act. Attacking mortals was most likely to do that. Not because mortals were valued more than immortals, but because harming mortals was more likely to draw the attention of other mortals, and the very worst sin they could commit was to bring their kind to the attention of mortals.

Her people had spent millennia hiding their existence. The world simply wasn't ready to learn that, while the fabled cursed and soulless vampire didn't exist, a more scientific version of the creature did. One pumped full of bioengineered nanos programmed to keep the immortal at their peak condition. It was those very nanos that forced them to seek blood from outside sources. The nanos used blood, not only to propel and clone themselves, but to fight any illnesses that attacked their hosts' bodies, and to make the repairs caused by injuries or the effects of the sun, or pollution, or the simple passage of time. The hosts' bodies simply couldn't supply the amount of blood the nanos used to do all that, so outside sources were necessary, which hadn't been a problem in their homeland when the nanos were first invented and introduced: blood transfusions had taken care of the problem. But when their home—the legendary Atlantis, an isolated land as technologically advanced as was whispered—fell, their people found themselves forced to flee and join the rest of the world. One where there was no such thing as real science, let alone nanos or blood transfusions.

Programmed to keep their hosts at their peak condition, the nanos had forced evolutionary changes on their people, bringing on fangs along with added strength, speed, and night vision to make them perfect predators, able to get what they needed to survive. Which had made the rest of the world their prey.

Much as most immortals didn't like to admit it, mortals were essentially cattle to Katricia's kind. Friends, neighbors, and cattle . . . Or at least they had been, for millennia. Blood banks had helped bring an end to that need to feed "off the hoof," as they had taken to calling it over time.

"Believe me, hunting rogues isn't nearly as exciting as it sounds," Katricia assured him with a wry smile as he picked up a card, situated it among the ones in his hand, and discarded another. "Actually, it's a lot of long hours of waiting, researching, checking data, and then a quick raid and clean-up. It gets tired pretty quick."

"Still, it's probably more interesting than being a small-town cop," Teddy assured her wryly as she took her turn. "Most of my job is made up of issuing tickets, picking up shoplifters, and the occasional domestic dispute." He smiled and then added dryly, "At least, it was. The last couple of years, though, we've actually had a couple of murder attempts, assaults, and arsons."

Katricia raised her eyebrows as he picked up a card. "And this started just the last couple of years?"

Teddy nodded and chuckled, his gaze on his cards as he shifted a couple. He discarded before saying, "Yes, since the vamps came to town."

Katricia's eyes widened. "You mean our people have been killing and—?"

"No," he assured her quickly. "Much to my dismay, it isn't the vampires committing the crimes but the mortals, and they're attacking the immortals," he admitted with disgust and shook his head before adding, "Mind you, in each one of those cases, those mortals would have claimed that the inoffensive vampire, or immortal, was the monster. It really makes you shake your head in wonder."

"Hmm," Katricia muttered, taking her turn. She didn't bother asking why the mortals had attacked the immortals. Her guess would be fear. People did the stupidest things out of fear. As she discarded, she asked, "So what is the job coming up?"

"Chief of police," he answered, picking up a card.

Katricia stared at him blankly as he discarded, and then pointed out, "But *you're* the police chief of Port Henry."

Teddy smiled faintly, and teased, "A top-notch detective, I see."

"Ha ha," Katricia said grimly. "Why would you need a replacement? You obviously love your job. Every time it's come up in conversation today—" She shrugged helplessly and finished, "I could tell you love it."

"I do," he agreed mildly, and then gestured for her to continue with her turn before pointing out solemnly, "But I'm getting old."

"You're not old," she said at once. "You're just a baby. Cripes, I'm ages older than you."

"I'm old for a mortal," Teddy said patiently. "Retirement is coming up. Someone will have to take my place. Someone who can deal with immortals would be

good and you could do that. I'll talk to Lucian and if
he thinks you can handle the job, we'll see what we
can—"

"I don't want your job, Teddy," Katricia said quietly, and it was true. She didn't want it. She also didn't
want him to give it up when he so obviously loved it.
And he wouldn't have to once she turned him, but she
couldn't tell him that. She frowned over that fact with
frustration and simply said, "I'd rather work with you
than take your place."

Teddy was silent for a moment, his eyes locked on
her briefly, and then he suddenly set down his cards
and stood. "I'm ready for a drink. How about you?"

Katricia set her cards down and got up as well, voice
eager as she asked, "Coffee again?"

Teddy chuckled, but shook his head as he moved
from the coffee table in front of the fireplace to the
kitchen. "Are you kidding? You were wired all day
from those two cups at breakfast. I give you coffee now
you won't sleep tonight."

"Sleep is overrated," Katricia said with forced good
cheer.

"Not for an old mortal guy like me, it isn't," he assured her wryly, retrieving a gift bag from the top of
the refrigerator.

"What's that?" Katricia asked curiously.

"Whiskey," Teddy answered, and proceeded to open the sealed bag. When he caught Katricia's raised eyebrows, he shrugged and pulled out the bottle inside, explaining, "It's the same thing every year. Twelve-year-old scotch."

Katricia nodded, but leaned around him to read the gift card as he retrieved two glasses from the cupboard. "Elvi? Uncle Victor's Elvi?"

Teddy grunted and poured some whiskey into each glass. "Elvi knows I like this whiskey. She gives it to me for Christmas every year and Mabel makes me cookies, a hat, scarf, and mitts. I drink the whiskey, eat the cookies, and even wear the hat and scarf, but the mitts . . ." He grimaced and shook his head.

"Mitts not your thing?" Katricia suggested with amusement, but her gaze was on his face as he set down the bottle and touched the tag on the gift bag, turning it so that he could peer at the signature. She couldn't help noting the soft affection of his expression. She'd also noted the emotion in his voice when he'd said Elvi's name. It had been different than when he'd said "Mabel," almost husky and warm and . . . and she didn't really like it, Katricia thought grimly.

"No, mitts aren't quite my thing," Teddy acknowledged, letting go of the gift tag to smile at her wryly. "Hard to pull the trigger on a gun with mitts on . . .

Not that I've even had to pull my gun more than a time or two over the years. Still, I should be prepared to if the occasion arises."

"I suppose," Katricia agreed quietly, taking the glass he now held out. The drink wouldn't affect her. The nanos in her body would prevent any intoxication. For immortals to enjoy that kind of thing even briefly, they had to actually consume the blood of an intoxicated mortal. Not that she wanted to experience intoxication, or thought it might be something enjoyable. Katricia liked to be in control of her faculties. Usually. Although, she thought that just then she might like to experience the effect alcohol had on mortals. She didn't like the jealousy presently coursing through her. It was an emotion she'd never experienced before . . . and she didn't feel at all comfortable experiencing it now. So, what did she do about that? Change the subject and try to forget it? Heck no, she downed her whiskey, allowed it a moment to burn its way down her throat and into her stomach, which was already churning with jealousy, and then asked the one thing sure to increase the burning jealousy in her gut. "Tell me about Elvi."

Teddy paused, his own glass halfway to his mouth, and simply stared at her blankly, obviously completely stunned by the question. "I— You— Why?"

"You've mentioned her several times today," Katricia said with a shrug. "Every time Port Henry came up, in fact. As if she's synonymous with the town."

"Well, she's . . . I suppose she and Mabel are kind of representative of the town to me," Teddy muttered, looking uncomfortable. "The three of us have been friends since we were kids. I stood up in both their weddings and . . ." He shrugged helplessly. "We've been friends a long time."

Her eyes narrowed as she noted the way he was avoiding her eyes. "Why did you never marry?"

"I just never found anyone I loved as mu— Anyone I loved," he corrected himself with a frown.

"You never found anyone you loved, or anyone you loved as much as Elvi?" Katricia asked dryly, not having missed the slip.

Teddy's mouth tightened. "It's getting late. Time for bed," he announced, turning to lift his glass and take a drink. He swallowed heavily and then added, his voice husky from the whiskey, "Grab one of the sleeping bags I brought out earlier. You can have the couch. I'll take the floor."

Katricia stared at him silently for a moment and then simply turned and left the living room to slip into the bathroom. While the fire and several candles had lit up the main room, she hadn't thought to bring a candle with her, and darkness closed around Katricia as soon as she closed the door. But between her night vision and the small bit of moonlight streaming through the window, she could see fine and peered at herself in the mirror, surprised to find her eyes hadn't turned green, after all.

Closing her eyes briefly, she forced herself to take several deep breaths, and reminded herself that Teddy was her life mate. That being the case, whatever he'd felt for Elvi in the past wouldn't matter. It would be nothing next to what he would experience with and feel for her in the future. The nanos were never wrong, and they had put him with her, not Elvi. Feeling herself relax, Katricia opened her eyes and peered at herself in the mirror. A plan began to form in her mind then, on how to begin to turn his attention from Elvi to her, one that brought a slow smile to her lips.

Teddy stared at the closed bathroom door and downed the rest of his whiskey. He usually enjoyed Elvi's gift, but tonight it tasted like ash in his mouth and he hadn't a clue why. Except that, for some reason, he felt incredibly guilty, as if his feelings for Elvi, feelings he'd had since he was a callow youth, were somehow betraying this new and very tentative friendship with Katricia . . . which was just stupid. He'd only met her today. And aside from her first flirting, there had been nothing untoward since, not even a hint of flirting from her—or him, for that matter. Instead, they'd seemed to bond, friendship growing between them as they'd played, talked, and worked together as a team.

It was something Teddy had never really experienced before. Oh, he'd had many female friends over the years and had worked toward a common goal with just as many. He'd worked with Mabel to try to find Elvi a mate, had planned and arranged local fairs with Elvi. But he'd never experienced the same level of ease and rightness with either of them as he had with Katricia. They'd seemed to communicate at times without needing to speak, and their working together in the kitchen had been almost like a dance. He felt closer to her after one day than he'd felt with women he'd been lovers with for months. Which was just strange, he decided and shook his head before turning to put the cap back on his whiskey and return it to the gift bag.

The bathroom door opened and Teddy watched silently as Katricia reappeared and grabbed one of the two sleeping bags he'd set on the chair beside the couch earlier. She then moved to the couch, unrolled and laid out the sleeping bag, unzipped it, and crawled inside. She didn't bother to zip it back up, he noted as he took the candle that he'd set on the kitchen counter earlier and headed for the bathroom himself.

The room was damned cold compared to the main room, and Teddy was quick about his ablutions. Within ten minutes he was back, blowing out candles and unrolling his sleeping bag in front of the fireplace. His gaze slid reluctantly to Katricia then, as he wondered if he should have offered her the spot in front of the fire. The couch would be more comfortable, but the floor in front of the fire would be warmer.

Finding her eyes closed, Teddy decided she would probably be warm enough in the sleeping bag and quickly unzipped his and started to get into it. Then, recalling he still wore his flannels under his clothes, and deciding he'd be more comfortable out of his jeans, he quickly shed them and his sweater, folded them neatly, set them aside, then got into his sleeping bag and quickly zipped it closed again. Within moments, his eyes were drifting shut.

Teddy wasn't sure how long he'd been sleeping when a whisper of sound brought his drowsy eyes open again to find Katricia kneeling beside him.

"What's wrong?" he murmured sleepily, trying to wake up fully.

"I'm cold," Katricia whispered. Before he quite knew what was happening, she'd opened the zipper to his sleeping bag and climbed in to join him, adding, "Share your body heat."

"You— I— We— This isn't—" he stammered, but his protests grew weaker with each attempt as her body slid against his inside the sleeping bag.

"I'm old enough to do what I wish. You're an adult, too. We want each other and this *definitely* is a good idea," she breathed, her body wrapping around his.

Teddy just gaped at her for a moment, stunned that she'd responded correctly to each of his aborted protests as if he'd spoken them aloud rather than stammered helplessly like a schoolboy. By the time he regathered his wits, she was wrapped around him like a warm, tight sleeping bag, her body pressing against his in several key places.

"You read my mind," he muttered, trying by sheer force of will to keep from reacting to her nearness. It seemed his will was weak. He was definitely reacting. Little Teddy had been up and down all day, but was fully up now.

Much to his surprise, Katricia chuckled at his accusation. He didn't understand, and it was hard to care much about what had amused her with her hands sliding around his back and her breasts and groin nestling up against him. She smelled so damned good, Teddy thought and then heard her say, "I can't read you, Teddy."

Despite his growing distraction, Teddy frowned. "What was that?"

"I said I can't read you," Katricia murmured, pressing a kiss to the bottom of his chin and then licking his throat before letting her lips drift to his cheek and then his ear.

"You can't read me?" Teddy muttered, his brain telling him this was important while the rest of his body was assuring him it really, really wasn't. Damn, she was squeezing his behind as if checking melons for firmness. Fortunately, he walked a lot on the job, making his rounds of the downtown businesses, and he knew he had a firm behind.

"No. I can't," she murmured, nibbling at his ear.

Teddy remained still for a minute. His brain was trying to decipher what that meant while the rest of his body was humming and thoroughly distracted with what she was doing. After a minute, he brought an end to her nibbles and squeezes by rolling her on her back inside the bag. He then rose up slightly to peer down at her face in the firelight. "You can't read me?"

Katricia blinked up at him in surprise in the firelight, and then realization crossed her face. It was followed by wariness and her mouth snapping closed.

"Am I your life mate?" he asked grimly.

Katricia bit her lip and glanced away, then sighed and shook her head and peered back at him. "I think so, yes."

The words took his breath away and Teddy simply gaped at her for a minute, but then asked slowly, "You think so? Or you know so?"

Katricia eyed Teddy for a moment. Marguerite's warning to go slowly was ringing in her head, but she just couldn't. She didn't even want to, and while she'd managed to behave all day, now that he was lying on top of her, his body feeling warm and solid despite it being a dream, and his erection nestled against her groin . . . Well, she just couldn't behave anymore. Spreading her legs so that he sank between them, his erection pressing more firmly where she wanted, Katricia let her hands slide over his back and down to his behind again to urge him more fully against her, and said, "I can't read you, haven't been interested in food for centuries before today, or sex for that matter. But I am now . . . and we're having a shared dream. Yes, you're my life mate."

Teddy stared at her for a moment, desire battling with a frown on his face, and then he asked, "This is a dream?"

That question really wasn't the reaction she'd expected. She hadn't really been sure what to expect, protestations maybe, the cut-and-run scenario Marguerite had got her worrying about. But this question left her unsure how he was reacting to the news. Biting her lip, Katricia nodded, and then gasped when he suddenly flung aside the top of the unzipped sleeping bag. Katricia's arms instinctively tightened around him to keep him from leaping up or rolling off of her.

But he didn't do either. Instead, Teddy bent his head and rubbed her nose with his, murmuring, "If it's a dream we don't have to worry about getting cold."

"No," she agreed in a whisper, her hold on him easing as he brushed his lips over hers. Katricia was almost sorry she'd loosened her hold when he suddenly shifted off of her, but he was only moving to lie next to her on the sleeping bag, and he continued to kiss her, just toying with her lips, brushing and then nipping at them. Teasing her, she decided and was about to open her mouth and deepen the kiss herself when he suddenly raised his head to peer down her body.

Teddy's eyes widened as he took in the over-large T-shirt that was her only covering, and he plucked at it lightly, one eyebrow rising. "Where did your clothes go?"

"This is what I normally sleep in," she whispered as his hand slid down her side to the outside of her upper thigh where the T-shirt ended.

"I like it," he announced. "Simple and sexy."

Her eyes widened and she bit her lip as his hand slid under the hem to ride up her outer leg to her hip. He watched his hand and wrist disappear under the cloth, and then shifted his gaze to her face and asked, "If this is a dream, why aren't I young and handsome for you?"

"You are young and handsome to me," she said huskily, and reached up to slip one hand around his neck. "I like you just the way you are. I find you sexy just as you are. I want you just as you are."

Teddy's eyes narrowed on hers, searching for the truth in her words and Katricia stared back. He was her life mate, the most beautiful man in the world to her. She didn't have to lie about that and met his gaze, unflinching, until his head lowered and his mouth covered hers. His hand continued upward then, skimming along the side of her waist and then gliding smoothly up to cover one breast under her T-shirt as his tongue thrust into her opening mouth.

Katricia moaned, her body arching as the double assault stirred hot desire to life in her. It raced through her like a forest fire, stronger than anything she'd ever experienced before, and she kissed him back with the desperation suddenly claiming her, her arms slipping around his shoulders and pulling him to half-cover her.

She ran her hands over the flannel covering his back, wishing it wasn't there, and suddenly it wasn't, and she was caressing his warm skin, her fingers gliding over shifting muscle.

When Teddy suddenly broke their kiss and removed his hand to pull away, Katricia's heart actually stopped beating briefly and she blurted, "Please don't run."

Teddy had been ducking his head, but paused and raised it to peer at her with surprise. "Run?"

Katricia nodded. "Marguerite warned me that I should let you get to know me better before I told you we were life mates. She said you might be overwhelmed if you knew too soon and might run. I—" She paused when he suddenly pressed a finger to her mouth to silence her.

"Tricia," he said solemnly. "I'm not running. I've seen what life mates can have. I've seen how good it can be between them, and never dreamed I'd be lucky enough to enjoy that. I have no intention of running."

"Oh." She peered at him uncertainly. "When you stopped kissing me, I thought . . ."

"You thought wrong," Teddy assured her firmly and then smiled and said, "I stopped kissing you to do this." He then ducked his head again, but this time managed to finish what he'd apparently intended when he'd broken their kiss. His clothes weren't the only thing now gone, her T-shirt was, too, leaving nothing to prevent his mouth closing over the nipple of the breast he'd been fondling.

"Oh," Katricia breathed as he sucked the nipple between his lips. She slid her fingers into his hair and arched into the caress.

He wasn't running. They would be life mates, she thought dazedly, legs shifting restlessly as he drew on her nipple. Christ, she didn't remember anything feeling this good when she'd still enjoyed sex. But then if it had, she probably wouldn't have tired of it, Katricia acknowledged, curling her fingers in his hair as he suckled her. When he let her nipple slip from his mouth and blew on the now-damp bud, she moaned and shifted beneath him, her back arching to invite him back. But instead of reclaiming it with his mouth, he covered it with his hand and kneaded gently as he raised his mouth to claim her lips instead.

Katricia opened to him at once, welcoming his tongue when it slid inside. Her hands then began moving over him, traveling his chest and exploring the wide, hard width. He might be older, but Teddy kept himself in good shape, and she squeezed the muscles of his chest, and then pinched at his nipples even as he pinched and tweaked hers. They both groaned in response and then Teddy released her breast and moved his hand to her hip to urge her on her side to face him fully before his fingers slid around to find and squeeze one butt cheek. Kneading and massaging the firm flesh, he urged her tighter against him and she felt his hardness against her thigh and then he suddenly released her behind and slipped his hand around between their bodies.

Katricia gave up on his chest and clutched at his shoulders with a gasp as his hand dipped between her legs. Just his one kiss and his brief caress had her so damp his fingers slid silkily against her hot, wet flesh. Katricia sucked on the tongue thrusting into her mouth and raised her leg to wrap it around his hip as she ground herself into his touch. Teddy took advantage of the room she gave him to maneuver and slid a finger inside her even as he continued to caress her with his thumb and Katricia broke their kiss on a cry, her body arching and straining upward. The action even shifted her several inches upward on the sleeping bag, but Teddy's hand simply followed and he lowered his mouth to her breast, laving the small globe, before sucking almost all of it into his mouth.

"Teddy," Katricia moaned. Need was a living thing inside her as she rode his hand, but she wanted his mouth on hers and him inside her, and . . . She wanted everything with a need that was almost frightening, and her voice was almost a growl as she pleaded, "Teddy, please. I need you inside me."

He immediately let her breast slip from his lips and shifted up to claim her mouth again, silencing her, but merely continuing to caress her. Moaning, Katricia immediately slid her hand down between them to find the hardness growing between them. But the moment she clasped him in hand, Teddy broke their kiss and stopped caressing her to catch her hand.

"Tricia, you really don't want to do that," he muttered, trying to force her hand away.

"Yes, I do," she assured him, tightening her hold and watching with fascination as his expression tightened along with it.

Groaning, Teddy shook his head and leaned his forehead on hers, muttering, "Sweetheart, I've been half-erect all damned day watching you run around in those damned tights of yours. It wouldn't take much to bring this to a premature end."

"Yoga pants," Katricia murmured, easing her grip a little.

"Huh?" He raised his head to stare at her blankly.

"They're yoga pants, not tights," she explained, nipping at his chin.

"Yoga?" Teddy echoed.

"Hmm." Katricia grinned at his expression and then whispered, "I'm very flexible."

"Damn," Teddy breathed, staring into her face. "This is going to be the poorest showing I've given since I was an eager teenager."

Katricia chuckled at his dismay and released his erection to slide her arms around his chest. "Then we'll just have to do it again and again. We have all night."

She saw his eyes widen, and then took him by surprise and turned him suddenly onto his back so that she could rise up to straddle him, but he was suddenly gone.

Five

Teddy grunted in pain and blinked his eyes open. He was still in his zipped-up sleeping bag, or mostly, his arm had escaped and he'd turned in his sleep and thumped it against the stone lip of the fireplace. It was the source of the pain radiating up his arm and what had woken him. Grimacing, he pulled the arm back into the sleeping bag and rubbed his wrist with his good hand, his eyes shooting to Katricia. She was still asleep on the couch, but her sleeping bag was undone and half off her.

He wondered briefly what was happening in the dream or if it had stopped with his waking, then tried to settle down to sleep again, eager to get back to it, but now that he was awake he was aware that the room was much colder than it had been when he'd fallen asleep.

Frowning, Teddy glanced to the fire to see that it had burned down to embers while they slept. He almost ignored it and went back to sleep anyway, but recalling that Katricia was farther away from the fire and half-uncovered, he reluctantly sat up and then slid from the sleeping bag to feed more logs to the fire. There were only two logs left, he saw with a frown. He hadn't noticed earlier they were running low or he would have fetched in more wood before retiring.

Teddy placed both logs in the fire and poked at them a bit, then straightened and quickly pulled on his jeans and sweater over his flannels. He then started to head over and get his coat, but paused beside the couch long enough to cover up Katricia. Immortals weren't affected by cold like mortals, but they were still affected. The nanos would be using up blood at an accelerated rate to fight the cold and Katricia couldn't afford that. As confident as she'd been that, snow or no snow, her blood delivery would come, it hadn't shown yet.

Katricia stirred sleepily as he tugged the sleeping bag back into place over her, and Teddy paused to peer at her for a moment. The dream was still fresh and clear in his mind, but it suddenly occurred to him to wonder if that wasn't all it had been. Maybe he just wanted to believe they were life mates and it had really just been all his own dream and not a shared one.

The thought was alarming. When she'd said it was a shared dream and they were life mates, he'd been happy to believe it. In fact, he'd eagerly embraced the news, knowing it meant having what both Mabel and Elvi had found: a relationship of earthshaking passion, complete trust, and deep binding friendship and love.

Teddy was too pragmatic to believe he loved Katricia already. It had only been a day, but he was pretty sure he was firmly headed that way. The woman was just . . . Well, she was sassy as hell, smart as a whip, and had a killer sense of humor. He'd laughed more today during their snowball fight, card games, and talks than he'd laughed with any woman ever.

She was also sexy as sin. He hadn't been kidding in the dream when he'd said he'd been half-erect all day. Every time he'd looked at her, little Teddy had perked up like a happy dog's ears. And he wouldn't have been surprised to hear his tongue had been hanging out half the day like that same happy dog's tongue. He'd never encountered a female who affected him like she did. Even Elvi.

The admission was a big one for Teddy. He'd been half in love with Ellen "Elvi" Black since he was a boy. No other woman had been able to compare, in his mind. Until now . . . and that was why he'd brought such an abrupt end to their conversation when Katricia had asked if he meant he'd never found anyone he loved, or anyone he'd loved as much as Elvi. Because he'd almost admitted, "Until now."

That thought in his head had startled the hell out of Teddy in that moment. But he now realized that, as much as he'd loved Elvi, it seemed to him it had been a young boy's love, a sort of adoration, but without the gritty lust he felt for Katricia. If he'd felt half as hot for Elvi as he did for Katricia, he wouldn't have simply stood by and watched her marry her mortal husband, and then he wouldn't have set out to find her a vampire mate. He'd have been desperate to claim her for his own. Teddy had always thought he'd stood aside for Elvi's sake, that he'd not wanted to stand in the way of her happiness. But the fact of the matter was, he suspected she'd just been an ideal to him. The perfect, untouchable female. He didn't even think he'd wanted her for real. Not like he wanted Katricia, because while he'd stood aside for Elvi, he already knew he couldn't do that with Katricia. He couldn't and wouldn't stand aside for her to find happiness with someone else . . . which would be a problem if they weren't really life mates and it had really all just been wishful dreaming on his part.

Sighing, Teddy ran one hand wearily through his hair, then turned and moved into the kitchen to grab his coat and boots. Rather than risk waking Katricia, he took them with him and slid out into the icy vestibule. He pulled the door silently closed before quickly donning them, and then grabbed one of the flashlights and slipped outside.

It had been cold that day, but it was even worse in the dead of night. The snow crunched under foot, the wind hit his face like icy sandpaper, and the moisture in his nose froze before he'd taken half a dozen steps. They definitely needed the wood, he thought grimly, and once he got back inside, he should probably set his watch alarm to go off every couple of hours so he could feed the fire again. In this kind of weather, they could freeze to death if the fire went out. Chances were the cold would wake him, but if it didn't . . . well, he didn't even want to think about that.

The tarp crinkled stiffly when he pulled it back to get to the wood it protected. Teddy quickly scooped up as many logs as he could carry and started back toward the cottage. He was nearly to the deck when he spotted light through the leafless trees between the cottage and the lakeshore in front of it. Pausing, he eyed it for a minute, then changed direction and walked around in front of the deck, traveling several feet down the gentle incline to get a better look without the trees in the way.

A slow smile curved Teddy's lips when he was able to see it clearly. A cottage across the lake was lit up like a Christmas tree, light shining from every window. It wasn't the fact that they had power that made him smile, but that there was someone else on the lake. Tomorrow morning he could walk across the frozen lake and ask to use the phone to take care of the power problem if it wasn't already taken care of by then. He might even be able to beg a ride into town for better provisions to get them by until the road was clear and they could drive out.

A loud rustling in the trees behind and to the side of him caught his ear. Teddy stiffened, and then slowly turned his head to peer over his shoulder. He spotted the large, lumbering shape by the shed and recognized it at once as a bear. There were few animals in the woods that size but bears. Seeing one of them at this time of year, though, was a rarity indeed. Bears didn't hibernate, as most people thought, at least not a true hibernation with the metabolic depression and lower body temperature. They actually slept and could be roused. Last night's storm had probably wakened the creature. A tree falling nearby its den or . . . Well, it could be anything, but whatever the case, the beast was up and probably hungry.

Teddy didn't panic right away. He was downwind and in the shadow of the trees. The bear wasn't likely to see or smell him and would, no doubt, lumber on his way after a moment or two. He just had to wait out the beast . . . and maybe pray the animal didn't lumber in his direction, he thought grimly, and then glanced sharply to the cottage when the door suddenly opened.

"Teddy?" Katricia called, stepping out onto the deck in her coat and boots and peering toward the shed. "Do you need help?"

Panic seized Teddy then. He didn't even think; seeing the bear pause and turn slowly in Katricia's direction, he let all but one of the logs he carried drop and started forward, roaring, "Get back inside!"

Katricia turned his way with surprise, but Teddy's attention was on the bear, who had turned and was now facing them both. The beast hesitated, and for one moment, Teddy had hope that the bear would be scared off by the sudden activity and noise. But it was mid-winter and the animal was hungry enough that noise and motion wouldn't put him off when there was a meal to be had. The bear charged.

"Get inside!" Teddy repeated, raising his log as he ran. He continued to shout as he raced forward, log upraised, making as much noise and trying to make himself as big and threatening as he could. The bear didn't even slow. It was like a game of chicken, but at the last moment, Teddy stepped to the right toward the cottage and swung for the side of the bear's head with all his might. He connected, the impact vibrating up his arms, but he hadn't stepped far enough or fast enough and felt the claws of one paw tear into his chest and stomach. Gasping in pain, he swung again even as he stumbled back against the cottage wall, managing to whack the beast in the snout as the bear turned toward him. The bear roared in pain and fury and rose up on his hind legs. Teddy was pretty sure he was done for when the sudden blast of a gun exploded to his side.

Startled, Teddy turned to find Katricia rushing down the stairs, his gun in hand, and pointing at the air as she loosed another bullet. He stared at her blankly, wondering how she'd got inside, grabbed his gun, and got back so fast, but then recalled immortals had incredible speed. He turned to peer back toward the bear, relieved to see the large back end of the beast disappearing into the trees. Apparently, the combination of his log and the gun was enough to make him decide against pursuing this meal.

"Are you all right?" Katricia was in front of him, the moonlight enough to reveal the concern on her face. "I smell blood. Did he get you?"

Teddy clutched the log in his hands, teeth gritting as he became aware of the burning in his chest, but merely shook his head. "Don't worry about it, I'm fine," he lied and turned away to move slowly toward the logs he'd dropped.

"Teddy, your coat's ripped," Katricia said, following. "Let me see—"

"I'm fine," he growled, waving her away. "We need to get the wood and get inside in case he changes his mind and comes back. You can look at it then."

Katricia hesitated, but then hurried past the stairs and the end of the deck to quickly gather up the logs he'd dropped to go after the bear. Teddy was relieved not to have to do it himself. Now that the panic was over, the adrenaline was beginning to seep out of him and he was starting to feel weak and shaky.

Leaving her to it, he stopped at the stairs and pressed the log he carried to his chest to free his other hand to hold the rail. He started up the four short steps, frowning at how much effort it took. By the last step, it was like climbing Mount Everest, and he was swaying, his hold on the rail the only thing keeping him upright.

"Teddy?" The concern in Katricia's voice made him straighten and force himself to take the two steps to the cottage door. He managed to pull it open and stagger inside. He even made it to the open inner door to the cottage, but then he was suddenly on his knees and slumping against the door frame, both arms now hugging the log to his chest, instinctively pressing it tight against the pain beginning to radiate there.

"Teddy!"

He heard the crash of the wood hitting the vestibule floor behind him and then Katricia was catching him under the arms. The log slipped from his hold and dropped to the floor as she lifted him to his feet from behind and propelled him out of the doorway and inside. The damned woman was practically carrying him like he weighed no more than a child, he thought with disgust as she moved him to a kitchen chair and set him in it. These immortal women could really be hard on a man's ego.

"Let me see." She moved around in front of him and tried to pluck his arms away from his chest, but he merely turned away on the seat with annoyance.

"Get the wood and close the door first. You're letting all the heat out," Teddy muttered.

Cursing, Katricia hurried to do as he said. The moment she did, he sagged back in the chair and let his arms drop away so he could peer down at himself. The only light in the room was the fire in the fireplace. The two logs he'd put on before going outside were now burning merrily, but it didn't really cast much light on the situation this far away. Still, he could make out enough to know he'd taken a serious injury.

He could see the wound was long, tearing through his heavy winter coat at the right side of his upper chest and shooting down at a diagonal to his left hip. The animal's claws had shredded through the cloth, insulation, and even the zipper . . . and, no doubt, his skin as well. He could see the sheen of blood in the dim light and was now aware of the dampness down his stomach and legs. His jeans were wet with his own blood, and liquid was trickling down his legs. Christ, he was bleeding badly, he thought with concern. And it was beginning to hurt like hell now.

"Let me see." Katricia was there again, turning the whole chair to face her, and this time Teddy didn't try to stop her.

Her reaction on first seeing the wound was a bit alarming. Immortals had better night vision than mortals, and he had no doubt she could see in this light as easily as if it were daylight. The dismay and horror on her face as she bent to look at his chest and stomach wasn't encouraging, and then she was suddenly all activity and curses as she quickly set about removing his coat.

"Why the hell did you do it?"

That frustrated mutter caught his ear as Katricia finished with his coat and started on his sweater, simply ripping the tattered material to the sides.

Opening eyes he hadn't realized he'd closed, Teddy frowned at the top of her head and asked with confusion, "Do what?"

"Attack the damned bear," she snapped, now rending the shredded flannel top of his pajamas open as well.

"I was trying to save you," he muttered, swallowing when he saw that his skin was torn just as the material had been. It looked damned deep, too. Four gouges running diagonally from chest to hip like long ditches in his body.

"I'm immortal. You should have let me handle him," Katricia snapped, suddenly straightening to move to the sink.

"Fine. Next time a bear's around and you come out bellowing like a female moose drawing its attention, I'll let the damned thing eat you," Teddy growled irritably as she returned with a dish towel. When she began to mop at his chest, he winced against the pain and ground out, "Are you sure you want to do that? You're wasting good blood. Maybe you should just lap it up while it's on offer."

When Katricia raised her head and glared at him, Teddy grimaced and then gave a slight shrug, which made him wince again as he said, "It's perfectly good blood and your delivery hasn't arrived yet. Besides, it runs all the way down my legs. Could be fun to have you lick it up. It would certainly distract me from the pain."

When her eyes widened incredulously, he closed his eyes and leaned his head back, muttering, "Ignore me. I think I'm delirious. Must be the aftereffects of that damned dream I had."

"We had," Katricia corrected solemnly and continued to mop at his chest.

Teddy struggled his eyes open and forced his head back up to stare at the top of her head again. "We?"

"It was a shared dream," she said without looking up, her concentration on trying to clean up enough blood to see the wound better, but the blood was still oozing out.

"A shared dream?" he echoed, a slow smile replacing the pain on his expression. "So we are life mates?"

Katricia merely nodded, her concentration on his wound, and Teddy grinned like an idiot for a moment, but then frowned and sighed.

"Well, doesn't that just figure? Turn out to be a life mate and die before I get to enjoy it," he muttered with disgust and then drew in a hissing breath when she gave up trying to clean away the blood and pressed the cloth firmly to his chest and stomach to try to stop the bleeding.

"You're not going to die," she said grimly, pressing harder on the wound. "I'll turn you. It will be fine."

"You need blood for a turn and there isn't any here. You can't turn me," Teddy said gently, and then forcing his head up and eyes open again, he took in the fear on her face and forced a smile. "Don't worry, I'm too ornery and stubborn to die."

Katricia didn't appear much reassured. Teddy supposed it was because his voice seemed to grow weaker with each word and they both knew they were empty anyway. He was pretty sure he was going to die. In fact, he was growing cold, which could be shock, but he suspected was loss of blood. He was bleeding out, Teddy thought, letting his eyes drift closed again.

"Maybe you should put another log on the fire. It's getting cold in here," he muttered wearily just before darkness claimed him.

Six

Teddy woke up warm in a bed with just a sheet covering him to the waist and a mess of blankets gathered below his feet where he'd kicked them off. This was how he was used to waking up. However, he didn't recognize the room he was in. The light was on, revealing soothing pale blue walls similar to his bedroom at home, but the furnishings were all wrong. The two dressers and bedside tables were all a light wood, the windows were covered by ice-blue blinds instead of his own, darker blue drapes, and the bed he was in was king-size and damned comfortable.

He also wasn't alone in the bed, Teddy noted, peering at the woman lying beside him in bed. Katricia in the overlarge T-shirt she'd been wearing in their shared dream. Even as he peered at her, she murmured sleepily and rolled toward him, flinging her arm over his chest, a chest that didn't have gray hair sprouting out of it, he realized and lifted his head to look himself over. His chest was wide, his pecs defined, his stomach flat and missing the bit of a pot belly he'd gained over the last couple of years as age crept up on him. Now his skin stretched tight over muscle and bone, and a light mat of dark hair had replaced the gray hair on his chest, as well as on his arms . . . and his legs, he saw, shifting one out from under the sheet. His arms and legs were also as taut and sculpted, as they'd been when he was younger.

And he wasn't feeling a single ache or pain. Normally, he woke up to a stiffness that settled in while he slept, and it took a bit of time and some moving around for that to pass. He wasn't suffering it now though. In fact, he felt damned good. Full of energy and . . . hell, he had a morning stiffy, too. Hadn't had one of those in a while, he thought with a grin.

That was when Teddy realized he was dreaming again. Must have passed out, he thought. He was probably still slouched in the kitchen chair with Katricia working over him, trying to save his life. It couldn't be a shared dream, because while Katricia was wearing the same T-shirt, he'd still been his sixty-four-year-old self, not the strong, healthy specimen he'd been as a soldier. So he had to be having his own dream now.

Either that or he was dead and this was heaven, Teddy supposed. He wouldn't have thought he could have Katricia with him in heaven, since she was probably still alive, but he guessed maybe you got what you wanted in heaven, and if so, this would be it. Katricia and a bed. Teddy was pretty sure that was definitely heaven for him.

The thought made him smile faintly. Just a day ago, he would have said that heaven to him would have been a nice walk through the woods with Elvi, like they used to do as teenagers. What a difference a day could make, he thought wryly and then glanced down to Katricia as she murmured sleepily and shifted her leg along his under the sheet. Her bare leg against his bare leg, he noted with interest. He wasn't the only one interested in this fact. Little Teddy showed his own fascination by perking up as if trying to look around under the sheet.

Teddy lowered the hand that had been resting up by his head and ran it lightly over Katricia's back on top of the T-shirt. The light touch made her sigh and start to roll into it, and he quickly lifted his arm away to keep it from being trapped against the bed as she rolled onto her back. When she then lay still, he eased onto his side and peered at her. She looked sweet and innocent in her sleep, with none of the wicked humor that often peeked out of her expression when she was teasing him. He actually kind of missed that. Teddy liked that streak of naughtiness in her, the sexy smiles, the teasing glint in the eyes as her gaze raked his body, the unapologetic glee in her expression as she hit him with a snowball or trounced him in cards. The uninhibited pleasure she had expressed over the simple fare they'd had to eat, and the pleasure they'd briefly experienced in their shared dream.

Katricia brought the young Teddy out in him, the man who enjoyed life and wasn't so burdened down with responsibilities. He'd grown cynical after years of being a cop, but she made him feel like the world could be a good place. She made him feel alive again . . . which was pretty ironic, since he was probably dead, he supposed. But it was hard to care much about that when he was here with her. Whether it was a dream or heaven, he didn't care. He was ready to enjoy it.

Smiling, Teddy plucked at the sheet covering them both from the waist down and drew it slowly away until her bare legs were revealed. He then kicked it off himself as well as he gazed over her. Teddy had noted before that she had an athlete's body, and now found himself unable to resist sliding his hand over the top of her near leg, starting just above the knee and running it up to the hem of her T-shirt where it ended at the top of her thighs.

Katricia breathed out a little sigh and shifted onto her side again, facing him as his fingers drifted over the taut, muscled leg.

She could have been a runner, he thought, moving his hand from the leg that was now closest to the bed and shifting it to rest on her upper leg. He slid it upward to her hip, pushing the T-shirt ahead of it, and his gaze skated over every inch of skin revealed as he continued to push the light cloth upward. It was large and loose, and he'd pushed the cloth up to the underside of her breast before she moaned and rolled onto her back.

Teddy followed, bending over her to claim the far nipple as his fingers pushed the cotton over the mound. He drew it between his lips and suckled at it, his eyes widening incredulously as the action sent pleasure tingling through his own body. It made him suckle harder, and then graze it with his teeth, which just intensified the sensations running through him, and he moaned, vaguely aware of Katricia releasing a sleepy moan of her own.

Releasing her nipple, he lifted his head to peer at her, but she was still asleep. Her mouth was parted now though, and her breathing was shallow. Watching her face, he slid his hand to her breast, covered it, and gently squeezed, then squeezed again before catching the nipple between thumb and forefinger and tweaking it lightly.

Katricia moaned again, her head turning on the pillow, and Teddy had to bite his lip to keep from moaning with her. Damn, he was experiencing her pleasure, he realized. Like a life mate was supposed to be able to do. This had to be heaven, he decided and lowered his head to her other breast and began to minister to it with his mouth as his hand released her first breast and slid down across her stomach to dip between her legs. She was warm and already wet. He wasn't surprised; little Teddy was certainly excited by the sensations coursing through them. The little trooper was already standing at attention, but straightened even more as Teddy slid his fingers over Katricia's damp skin, sending shaft after shaft of pleasure through them both, exciting them further.

Teddy had been with a lot of women in his day and had always considered himself a generous lover, but damn, he hadn't realized just how good he was. It was no damned wonder he'd never wanted for female companionship.

The arrogant thought ran through his head as he let his mouth explore her body, laving and nipping his way from one breast to the other, but he stopped thinking altogether and simply allowed himself to feel and experience as his mouth followed the path his hand had taken and began to lick its way down her stomach.

Katricia woke up gasping for air and making little panting squeaks of sound. Her body was burning up from a fire centered between her legs. For one moment, she simply lay there, staring at the ceiling of the bedroom in her cousin's cottage as wave after wave of passion poured over her, but then she recalled how she'd got there and why and concern pushed enough of the passion aside to allow her to look for Teddy.

She supposed she shouldn't have been surprised to find his head buried between her legs, causing the fire eating her alive; nothing and no one else had made her burn like he did. But Katricia was surprised. She'd sat up with him for more than twenty-four hours as he'd gone through the turn, feeding him bag after bag of blood to get him through it, terrified through most of it that between his age, the injury he'd sustained, and the amount of blood he'd lost he wouldn't survive. When the worst of it was over and he still lived, Katricia had finally allowed herself to sleep, but she'd climbed into bed next to him to be sure he didn't wake up alone and confused. The last thing she'd expected was to find him—

"Oh God," she gasped, her thoughts scattering as Teddy pushed a finger up into her even as he continued with what he was doing. The pleasure that rolled through her then was so overwhelming it was almost terrifying. It was too much. She couldn't—

"Teddy!" Katricia cried, grabbing his hair and tugging almost viciously in her desperation to make him stop. She couldn't catch her breath and felt like she was drowning in the pleasure he was causing. It was slamming through her body and crashing into her brain in repeated, pitiless waves, and then he responded to her tugging, stopped what he was doing, and rose up, moving up her body. But her respite was short-lived, because then he was sliding into her even as his lips claimed hers.

Katricia groaned into his mouth. It had been a long time since anyone had been inside her body and he felt so damned good there. Her arms and legs wrapped around his shoulders and hips, and she held on for dear life as he thrust into her. If she was going to drown, at least she wouldn't go alone, Katricia thought, clinging to him with everything she had, even her lips. Her mouth was almost suctioned to his until he broke their kiss and moved his lips to her ear, muttering, "You smell so damned good."

Katricia merely groaned and nuzzled his ear back, nipping at it as his body pounded into hers. When she felt his teeth sink into her neck, her eyes blinked open with surprise, and then she screamed as a final, redoubled wave of pleasure crashed through her, a tsunami that rolled through her mind, dragging it under to the murky depths.

Katricia woke up some time later and opened her eyes to find herself peering over a blood bag at Justin Bricker's smiling face. Frowning around the bag in her mouth, she half sat up, and then paused to catch the sheet that started to slip off of her naked body. Glancing around, she saw Teddy lying on his back next to her, with Anders holding a bag to his mouth as well. He was still unconscious.

"You let him bite you."

Katricia turned to peer at Bricker at that comment. He actually tsked as he said it, and she scowled at him around the bag. She hadn't let Teddy bite her, he'd caught her by surprise. Not that she'd minded. It had been . . . well . . .

"Well, indeed," Bricker said dryly, obviously reading her mind. "But he's new to this and doesn't know when to stop biting. You'll have to explain that it's not good to bite until his turn is done. And then when he does bite, it should be more of a love bite than an actual bite-and-suck. Cripes, he must have taken a quart from you before he lost consciousness. You were both dead to the world when we checked on you and this is the third bag of blood I've given you."

Katricia frowned at this news, and then, realizing the bag was empty, tore it from her mouth and glanced to Teddy again, asking, "Is he all right?"

"He'll be fine. He just needs a couple more bags and he should be good," Bricker said soothingly, handing her another bag. "He's still turning, and taking in your nanos when he bit you . . . Well, you know that's not good."

Katricia nodded and slapped the bag of blood to her fangs. Every immortal had a certain number of nanos in their body, the perfect amount to keep them at their peak condition. It was the first things the nanos did on entering a new host: they assessed the situation and began to use up blood to reproduce, while at the same time repairing any life-threatening injury the host might have, and then they started right into the major changes. It was a painful process, and she'd had to watch Teddy writhe and scream for nearly a full night and day as he went through the worst of it.

But Teddy wasn't fully through the turn yet. There were still changes to be made in his body and it would continue for several days or even weeks. During that time, he would need extra blood to sustain the changes . . . and adding to that burden wasn't good. That was what Teddy had done by biting her. He'd taken her nanos into his body. Suddenly infusing himself with more of them had forced his own nanos to work extra hard to process them, using extra blood. In the meantime, until eradicated, the extra nanos had been using up blood as well. This wasn't a good thing for any immortal, really, but it was very bad for a new turn still in the process.

As for her, he'd definitely taken an unhealthy amount of blood from her if she'd needed three bags to even regain consciousness. She would have to explain these things to him so he didn't do it again while they were alone. It wouldn't have killed them, but it would have left them incapacitated until someone came along and found them. Fortunately, Bricker and Anders were still here to assist them this time, but—

"He's coming around."

Katricia glanced to Anders at that announcement to see him removing the latest bag from Teddy's mouth. Her gaze slid over Teddy's face, noting that his eyelids were twitching as if his eyes were moving under them.

"It's late. Nearly dawn. Is there anything you want before we retire?" Bricker asked, taking her empty bag from her when she removed it from her teeth.

Katricia shook her head and forced her eyes away from Teddy to offer the two men a smile as they moved to the foot of the bed. "No. Thank you, though."

Bricker nodded and turned to lead the way to the door, saying, "We'll leave the cooler here for now in case you need it again. We'll check with you before we leave at sunset."

Katricia nodded, but her eyes had already returned to Teddy and she heard rather than saw the two men leave the room. The sound of the door closing was what brought Teddy's eyes open. He peered at her blankly for a moment, and then glanced around the room with a moment's confusion before relaxing.

"For a minute I forgot," he admitted wryly, sitting up beside her.

"Forgot what?" Katricia asked uncertainly as he leaned to press a kiss to her shoulder.

"That I was dead," he murmured, following his kiss up with a nip before moving his lips to her ear.

"Dead?" she asked, pulling back with surprise.

"Mmm," he murmured, simply following to continue.

"But Teddy, you're not dead," Katricia said on a half-breathless laugh.

"Yes I am. And this is heaven," he assured her, turning his head to claim her lips now.

For a minute, Katricia simply couldn't speak. It was hard to speak with two tongues in your mouth, but when his hands began to roam over her body, she forced herself to break their kiss and pull back. Her voice firm, she said, "Teddy, you're not dead. This isn't heaven. I— Why would you think this was heaven?" she interrupted herself to ask suddenly.

"You, me, and a bed? It's heaven," he argued, nibbling on her ear again.

"You, me, and a bed, and not you and Elvi?" she asked with surprise.

Teddy pulled back to peer at her with amusement. "Do you see Elvi here? We didn't have that kind of relationship. She was . . ." He paused for a moment, as if searching for the words, and then frowned, his gaze sliding to her as he said, "Hey, this is my version of heaven. How come you get to ruin it with talk?"

"Because it isn't heaven," Katricia said firmly. "Now finish what you were saying. What was Elvi to you?"

He scowled at the question, his silver-gray eyes flashing with irritation, and then sighed and dropped back in the bed. "Fine. Elvi was . . . well she was kind of the ideal woman. The good girl, the good wife, the good mother. She was . . . good," Teddy finished helplessly, and then grimaced and added dryly, "Probably still is I guess. I'm the one who's dead."

"You're not dead," Katricia repeated, but her words were distracted, her thoughts on what he'd just said. "So, she was good. Kind of like a Madonna figure to you? Not—"

"Not a real woman like you," he interrupted, sitting up impatiently. "Now can we get back to my heaven?"

"No, wait," she said, pulling back when he reached for her again. "What's a real woman to you?"

Teddy sighed with resignation. "Someone who fires your blood, challenges your mind, keeps you on your toes, and has your back. A partner in every sense of the word."

"And you think I'm that? Already?" Katricia asked with surprise.

"I know you are," he said simply and when she just stared at him, he shook his head and said, "Who scared the bear off when I was battling him?"

"Me," she said with a frown.

"Another woman would have run inside and watched through the window while I took care of business. But you had my back and you used your brain to do it," Teddy pointed out with a nod, and then asked, "Who brained me with a snowball, and then smacked me with a dish towel and splashed me with water while we were doing dishes and just basically took every opportunity to have at me in a playful manner?"

"Ah," Katricia murmured, biting her lip guiltily.

"You keep me on my toes," Teddy said with a grin for her discomfort. "You have a sharp mind and are quick with comebacks. I don't know how many times today you won debates let alone card games."

"And I fire your blood," she whispered.

He nodded solemnly. "Yes, ma'am, you surely do. Little Teddy's been doing calisthenics all day since meeting you and he hasn't been this active in a very long time. Now, can we stop all this touchy-feely talking stuff and give him the workout he's begging for?"

"Begging for?" Katricia asked with husky amusement.

"Yes, begging, and if you don't mind my saying so I don't think I should have to beg in heaven."

"Teddy," she said with exasperation, clasping his face in both hands. "You are not dead. I turned you."

He stared at her for a full moment, expression blank, and then blinked and asked, "Turned me?"

She nodded apologetically and rushed out, "I know I should have asked you first, but you were dying. I couldn't let that happen. And your only protest when I brought it up was blood, so I turned you."

His eyebrows rose, and then he pulled his face free of her hands and glanced around. "But this room. It's not—"

"This is the master bedroom of Decker's cottage. The cottage next door to yours," she added in explanation. "It's my cousin, Decker's. Bricker and Anders helped me bring you here after the turn."

"Bricker and Anders?" Teddy asked with a frown. "I know Anders. He's an enforcer. But who's Bricker?"

"Bricker's an enforcer, too," she explained and then added, "When you passed out I called Aunt Marguerite. I was in a panic. You were dying and I needed to turn you, but the blood hadn't arrived yet. Fortunately, the blood courier arrived on snowmobile with the blood, gas, and food while I was talking to her. I turned you and he helped me strap you to the kitchen table to keep you from hurting yourself and then stayed to help watch over you until Bricker and Anders arrived. Lucian sent them up. Marguerite called him as soon as I hung up, and he arranged for them to bring more blood, men to clear the trees away, and a snow mover to clear the road so that the men could work on the power lines."

"The power's on," Teddy said with realization, lifting his gaze to the light on overhead.

Katricia nodded. "It was on by the time the worst of your turn was over. In both cottages."

"Then why bring me?" he asked with a frown.

"Because this one has the generator and there's gas now. Another storm is supposed to hit tonight. If the power goes out again, we'll still be good here."

"Smart," he murmured, smiling at her.

Katricia smiled back. "I thought so."

Teddy reached up to caress her cheek, but paused when he saw his hand. He released her and turned it over in front of his face, inspecting it. "No wrinkles, no liver spots."

"You're at your peak," Katricia said gently. "Your body is that of a twenty-five-year-old."

He nodded absently, his gaze dropping to his chest and legs, and then he glanced around the room until his gaze landed on the dresser mirror. He stared at their reflection silently and she turned to look, too, seeing the two of them reflected side by side on the bed, a young-looking blond woman and an equally young-looking dark-haired male. She was startled though when he suddenly lunged off the bed and walked over to stand in front of the mirror, then leaned in to look more closely at his face.

Katricia hesitated, then followed, shifting off the bed to walk up behind him.

"Christ, I haven't seen this guy looking back at me from the mirror in decades," Teddy muttered, running one hand over the dark stubble on his cheeks and leaning in closer to examine his eyes. "My eyes are silver."

"They were gray before the turn, they're silver-gray now," Katricia murmured, sliding her arms around his waist from behind as he straightened.

"My hair's fuller again, too," Teddy murmured, covering her hands with his, then pulling them apart to use one to tug her around in front of him. She thought he meant to pull her into his arms, but he turned her so her back was to him, and then slid his own arms around her waist to hold her in place in front of him so they could peer at their reflections. She was peering at his face, but could see his eyes moving down on the mirror traveling over her body in the reflection.

"I like your body," he said suddenly.

Katricia actually felt herself blush, saw it, too, and found it rather surprising. She'd thought herself well beyond blushing by now. She'd also thought she didn't have any body issues, but suddenly blurted, "My breasts are small."

His hands left her waist to travel up and close over the small globes and he growled, "They're perfect."

Katricia arched slightly at his touch, her body grinding against the growing hardness pressing against her bottom as he squeezed and kneaded her breasts, and then he concentrated on the nipples, running his fingers over the stiffening tips before catching and squeezing them gently.

"I love the sounds you make," Teddy muttered, lowering his head to kiss her neck.

Katricia blinked open eyes she hadn't realized she'd closed and gasped, "What sounds?"

In response, Teddy let one hand drop away from her breast to slide down between her legs and Katricia gasped, then groaned and pressed harder back against him as he began to caress her there.

"Those sounds," he whispered, licking her neck.

Feeling his fangs scrape her skin, she moaned, "No biting."

"Hmm?" he asked, slipping one finger inside her.

"No biting," Katricia gasped out, covering his hand with hers and managing, "It's— It's just bad for you. I'll explain why later."

"No biting," Teddy agreed, and then suddenly retrieved his hand from between her legs to scoop her up and carry her to the bed. He set her down on it, but didn't immediately follow her down. Instead, he caught one foot and raised it to press a kiss to her instep. He then nipped at it, his other hand sliding up her calf to rest behind her knee. "I like your legs too. They're strong and shapely."

"Oh," Katricia said breathlessly as his lips followed the path his hand had, sliding up the side of her calf. She gasped and writhed a little when he then dipped his head to lick at the back of her knee.

"You like that," Teddy growled and licked at the crease again, making her writhe some more. Smiling, he slowly let her leg lower, only to raise the other. "This shared-pleasure business is the bomb, as the kids back home would say."

Katricia gave a breathless laugh, but bit her lip as he licked behind that knee as well, sending up a whole new flutter of pleasure through her.

"What else do you like?" he asked, arching his eyebrow in question and letting the fingers of one hand skate along her thigh.

"Come here and I'll tell you," she whispered, holding up her hands.

Teddy hesitated, but then set her leg back down and climbed on the bed, crawling up between her legs. He slowed as his face drew level with the apex of her thighs, but she caught his arms and urged him to continue up until he knelt on all fours over her, with his knees between her legs and his hands bracing him on either side of her shoulders.

"Tell me what you like," he whispered, bending his head and ducking slightly to lick teasingly at the nipple of one breast.

"I like you," Katricia said simply, and then swept her leg against his knees, and raised her hand to push on his one shoulder, knocking him off balance. He fell to the

bed beside her with a startled "oomph" and she immediately rolled and then rose up to straddle him. Katricia
came to rest with his manhood pressed flat to his stomach beneath her and grinned wickedly at his surprised
expression as she challenged, "What do you like?"

Teddy smiled, then caught her at the hips and slid
her forward along his length and back, caressing them
both with the move. "I like whipped cream."

Katricia blinked in confusion, her hands reaching to
clasp his arms to steady herself as he slid her along his
body again. Gasping at the pleasure shooting through
her, she asked uncertainly, "Whipped cream?"

"Mmm." He raised one hand to caress a breast,
adding, "I'd like to spread it all over your body and lick
it off." Teddy then grinned and added, "Don't need to
worry about my high cholesterol now."

Katricia laughed breathlessly, and arched into his
touch, sliding herself over the hardness she rested on.
But her amusement faded quickly, and she groaned
when his other hand slid between them for a more tar-
geted caress. She closed her eyes briefly as he touched
her, but then lifted herself slightly and reached down
to guide him into her before settling back down with a
long groan that he echoed.

"Christ, Katricia, you feel so damned good," Teddy
growled as he was buried inside her to the hilt.

"So do you," she breathed, raising and lowering herself again, and then he released her breasts and gave up caressing her to catch her by the arms and drag her down to claim her mouth. Katricia kissed him back, her hips still moving on him, her nipples tightening even further as they brushed across the coarse hairs of his chest, and then he rolled them both, coming out on top. Teddy broke their kiss then and rose up slightly, his hand reaching for her one leg. Catching her behind the calf, he lifted it and brought it in front of him so that her ankle was by his face, then held on to her thigh and kissed her instep as he continued to thrust into her, pounding into her with a need that was almost violent.

Katricia immediately wrapped her other leg around his hips to help, and then grabbed the bedsheets and tore at them as he drove them both the few short steps needed before satisfaction and unconsciousness claimed them.

Seven

Teddy woke up to find Katricia curled up against him, her head nestled on his chest and eyes open as she drew invisible little figures on his stomach with the tip of her finger. He didn't know how she knew he was awake, but a heartbeat after he opened his eyes she stopped skin-sketching and tilted her head to peer up at him.

"Hello," she whispered, smiling.

"Hello," Teddy murmured and slid his arms around to catch her shoulders and pull her up for a kiss, but paused as he became aware of a bad taste in his mouth. Morning breath . . . or afternoon or evening breath. He wasn't sure which, since he had no idea what time it was. Whatever kind of breath it was it was bad, he decided with a grimace, and rather than use his hold on

her to pull her up for a kiss, he used it to set her aside
and quickly sat up and slid out of bed.

"Did you bring my stuff over?" he asked, but spotted his suitcase on the floor beside the dresser even as
he asked the question, and moved to it.

"What are you doing?" Katricia asked.

Teddy glanced over to see her sitting up, watching
him as he opened the suitcase. He turned back to dig
through it, answering, "Looking for my toothbrush
and toothpaste so I can clean my teeth and then kiss
you."

Katricia chuckled and he heard the rustle of her
standing up, and then her legs appeared beside him.
The sight of them made him pause so he could peer at
them admiringly.

"You have legs like a young colt," he murmured,
one hand instinctively moving to slide up the smooth
skin of one inner thigh. Katricia shifted toward him
then, her thighs parting a little, and Teddy leaned forward to press a kiss to the soft, fair hair between her
legs. When she sighed, her fingers sliding into his hair,
he started to urge her legs farther apart and angled his
head to dip between them, but caught himself at the
last minute.

"Toothbrush," he muttered, turning away to continue his search. She might not care if he had bad breath while kissing her there, but eventually he'd want to kiss her lips and she'd mind then. Honestly, it tasted like something had crawled into his mouth while he was sleeping and died there.

"I put it in the side pocket when I fetched it from the bathroom at the other cottage," Katricia said helpfully, bending to retrieve it for him. The action put her breast right in front of his face and Teddy couldn't resist leaning forward to catch the nipple in his mouth.

Katricia stilled and moaned at the caress, her hand gliding into his hair again, and Teddy turned, catching her arms to take her with him and then urged her to squat before him so that she didn't have to stay bent over. The position left her on her toes with her bent knees on either side of his legs and Teddy couldn't resist reaching to caress what she'd unavoidably opened to him. His caress brought a deep groan from Katricia. When she teetered on her toes, he slid his other hand around to hold her by the behind and help her keep her balance as he caressed her, then let the first breast slip from his mouth to move to the other, muttering, "I can see I'm not going to get much done for a while with you around."

"How long is your vacation before you have to return to Port Henry?" Katricia asked breathlessly as he claimed and began to lave the other nipple. The question made Teddy freeze.

Frowning now, he pulled back and muttered, "Forever, I guess."

Katricia blinked in confusion. "What?"

A bit distressed at the realization that had just struck him, Teddy shook his head, took the toothbrush and toothpaste she'd retrieved and still clutched in hand, then got to his feet, urging her up with him.

"I need to brush my teeth," he said distractedly and moved around her, only to pause uncertainly. He had no idea where the bathroom was. His gaze slid around the room. There were three doors in the room, one was a set of double doors, obviously the closet, but there were two other doors along one wall, one on either end. One, no doubt, led to the rest of the house, but the other might be a bathroom, he thought and tried the door on the right, relieved when it opened up into an en suite bathroom. He found the light switch, flipped it on, and then moved into the room. His gaze landed on the shower as he moved in front of the sink and he decided a shower was probably a good idea, too.

Teddy opened the toothpaste, squirted some onto his toothbrush, and was brushing his teeth when Katricia followed him into the room. She waited patiently as he brushed his teeth and tongue and rinsed. But when he turned off the tap and moved to the shower to turn on the taps, she asked, "Teddy? What do you mean forever?"

"I mean I can hardly go back as I am," he said quietly, adjusting the taps until he had the temperature where he wanted it. Stepping into the shower then, Teddy caught her hand and tugged her under the spray with him, adding, "It would be a little hard to explain my suddenly youthful appearance."

The realization was a rather distressing one to him. He'd expected he'd have another year as police chief of Port Henry and then he'd retire to live out the rest of his days in the small town where he'd been born, raised, and lived most of his life.

"But why?" Katricia asked with true bewilderment as he picked up the soap and began to rub it between his hands to create lather. "I mean I thought the people in Port Henry knew about our kind?"

Her words ended on a gasp as he began to run his soapy hands over her body. Teddy smiled faintly at how her nipples immediately pebbled up and her breathing became rapid and shallow at the simple touch. This life-mate business was some pretty powerful mojo. The worst lover in the world would be a star with this backing him, he thought. Fortunately, he was nowhere near a bad lover. At least he didn't think he was. He could be wrong, of course, Teddy acknowledged, finishing with her chest and letting his hands move down over her stomach before one slid around to her behind while the other slipped between her legs. He didn't dally there long. Touching her was exciting both of them and he had no desire to pass out in the shower.

"Teddy," she said, framing his face with her hands when he withdrew his hands to grab the soap again. "Don't the people in Port Henry know? I thought they did."

Sighing, he quickly built up more lather and began to wash himself as he admitted, "Some people in Port Henry do know. Some don't. The ones who know would be all right, but as police chief I serve all of them. I couldn't keep this a secret."

They both fell silent then. He was busy soaping himself up now and Katricia had picked up the shampoo to wash her hair. Teddy had no idea what she was thinking, but he was thinking he didn't have a damned clue what he was supposed to do now. He'd been a cop most of his life and police chief of Port Henry for almost half his life. It had been a nice steady paycheck and he'd socked money away for his retirement, but not enough to carry them through several centuries or even a millennia or two. Besides, he liked working. He liked having a reason to get up in the morning and—His thoughts died abruptly as he realized he'd have to avoid getting up in the morning from now on. Immortals avoided the sun, as a rule . . . well, except in the winter, when they were all bundled up against it, he thought as he poured some shampoo into his own hand to wash his hair and watched Katricia rinse hers.

"But you love that job," Katricia said suddenly as she finished rinsing off and moved out of the spray.

"I do. But I'll find something else I love," Teddy said quietly as he switched places with her to rinse the soap from his own hair and body. Then he closed his eyes and let the water rinse the soap away. He wished it could as easily rinse away the sudden depression settling over him. He was grateful as hell to be a life mate, to have a chance at all the joy and happiness Katricia and he could have together, but suddenly finding himself unemployed was a bit distressing.

Teddy heard the shower door open and close and knew Katricia had left the glass enclosure. Somehow it felt as cold and depressing as his thoughts, without her in there. Sighing, he turned and shut off the taps.

"You might not have to find something else," Katricia said quietly, handing him a towel as he stepped out.

Teddy took the towel, but then simply held it and watched her dry herself with her own. "How's that?"

"There's a way you can still be police chief of Port Henry," she said, running the terry cloth briskly over her body, and then she bit her lip briefly before saying,

"But to keep it, Teddy Brunswick might have to have a heart attack and die on his Christmas vacation up north."

Teddy was so startled he dropped the towel he was holding. Eyes wide, he asked, "What?"

"Teddy Brunswick would have to die and you'd have to return with a different name," Katricia said, pausing to peer at him solemnly.

He stared back silently, considering the suggestion, but then shook his head. "I couldn't just walk in and take over the job under a new name, Katricia. There are hiring processes and paperwork and I don't have any I.D. except my own, which says I'm sixty-four, and—"

"Lucian would see to it," she interrupted quietly, beginning to dry him off now. "We have people who take care of this kind of thing, Teddy. You could be supplied with new I.D. and the appropriate background. Then a little mind-control here and a little finessing there and voilà, you could be Teddy Argeneau, the new, young police chief of Port Henry."

"Teddy Argeneau, huh?" he asked with amusement, tugging the towel from her hand and dropping it on the floor as he pulled her against him.

"Or Teddy Smith or Johnson, or even John Hancock," she said, leaning against him and wrapping her arms around his shoulders. "Whatever you want. I just like Teddy because it's how I think of you now, and I picked Argeneau because it's my name. We could switch back and forth between Argeneau and Brunswick over the decades, or choose another name altogether. I don't care. But you could keep the job you love."

"But won't people recognize it's me?" he asked quietly.

"The ones who know about immortals will, and can be told the truth. But the ones who don't know won't recognize you. People see what they expect to see, Teddy," she said solemnly. "And they won't expect to see Teddy Brunswick, forty years younger."

"Hmm." He smiled, his body relaxing, and then bent to nuzzle the side of her neck. "I could have you and the job I love, too, in the town I love. Nice."

Katricia smiled and pulled from his arms, then caught his hand and led him back into the bedroom and straight to the bed. She let go of him then and started to crawl onto it, but stopped and glanced over her shoulder with a yelp of surprise at a sharp nip on her behind. Her eyes widened incredulously when she saw Teddy straightening from biting her butt cheek.

"I've wanted to do that ever since first seeing you in those damned leotards of yours," he admitted with a grin, one hand at her waist to hold her in place as he used his other hand to rub the spot soothingly.

"Yoga pants," Katricia corrected with an arched eyebrow, but his biting her reminded her that he would still need a lot of blood, and she shifted and turned at the same time, escaping his hold to sit on her behind and slide to the edge of the bed. "You probably need more blood about now. We should feed."

Teddy grimaced at the thought and stepped between her legs to prevent her from getting up. "Later. I have other, more pressing hungers right now," he assured her, and pressed the proof of those hungers against her.

Katricia wiggled against his hardness, but avoided his mouth when he tried to kiss her. Managing to catch him by surprise, she pushed him away to slip off the bed.

"I forgot to brush my teeth," she announced, moving to the cooler to retrieve a bag of blood. Tossing it to him, Katricia then turned and skipped quickly into the bathroom.

Her toothbrush was there beside the sink where she'd placed it the day she'd arrived, and she'd squirted toothpaste on it and begun to brush her teeth when Teddy suddenly appeared behind her in the bathroom mirror, the bag of blood still in his hand.

"I don't know how to . . . er . . . well, my fangs don't seem to want to— Do I have fangs?" he finished with a frown.

A strand of dark hair had flopped onto his forehead and he looked so bewildered and heartbreakingly
young that Katricia smiled around her toothbrush, but
merely nodded and quickly finished brushing and then
rinsed. She then turned to face him.

"There are two ways to bring them on until you
learn to control your fangs," she announced.

"How's that?" Teddy asked warily.

"I could bite or cut myself or you. The smell of
blood will usually bring them on," she explained, but
he grimaced at the suggestion.

"I'd rather you didn't hurt yourself or me. What's
the other way?" he asked.

Katricia hesitated, but then decided it would be more
fun to show him than to explain and simply dropped to
her knees in front of him.

"What—?" he began with surprise, and then
sucked in a hissing breath as she took little Teddy in
hand.

"Excitement will bring on your fangs, too," she said
with a grin, and then took no-longer-so-little Teddy
into her mouth to show him.

Katricia opened her eyes to find Teddy leaning over
her, simply staring down at her face. She smiled uncertainly up at him and whispered, "Hi."

"Hi yourself," he said with a grin, but when she reached for his head, he caught her hand and asked, "How old are you?"

Katricia stilled and blinked, but answered solemnly, "I was born in 411 AD."

She then waited nervously for his reaction, worried about how he'd take that news, but he considered it for a minute, then smiled and said, "Sweet sixteen, this year, huh?"

"Sixteen centuries," she agreed with amusement.

Teddy grinned and bent to kiss her lightly, then murmured, "Don't worry, you don't look a day over fifteen centuries."

Katricia gasped at the words, then swatted his arm and rolled him onto his back. She came up on top of him scowling, and began to poke him in the stomach and ribs, but he just chuckled and caught her wrists. Holding on to them, he tugged her down until her breasts rested against his chest and he could reach her lips. Then he kissed her passionately, his hips moving under her so that she felt the hardness pressing against her.

By the time he broke the kiss, they were both breathing heavily, so Katricia was a little surprised when he nibbled at her ear briefly before asking, "When is your birthday?"

"December twenty-fifth," she answered breath-lessly, and then gasped in surprise when he suddenly rolled her off of him and rose up over her.

"Christmas Day?" Teddy asked with dismay.

Katricia nodded uncertainly. "Yes."

"Damn."

Much to her amazement, he was suddenly off the bed. Katricia sat up and stared at him where he'd gone to rifle through his suitcase. When he retrieved a pair of jeans and began to drag them on, she frowned and asked with confusion, "What are you doing?"

"Getting dressed," he said, doing up his jeans and frowning when he found them a little loose. Shaking his head, he dug out a sweater next and asked, "Those fellows who came to help out didn't happen to clean off my pickup, did they?"

"Teddy—"

"It doesn't matter. If they didn't, I'll clear away the snow myself. What are you doing?" he asked, paus-ing to frown at her where she still sat on the bed. "Get up. Get dressed. We have to go to town. You—" He stopped and blinked several times, then shook his head. "On second thought, don't. It's better if you wait here anyway. I won't be long."

"Teddy," she said with exasperation as he hurried for the door to the hall. She started to slide off the bed, but paused when he swung back halfway there. He wasn't responding to her voice, however, he simply rushed back to his suitcase for socks. Straightening with them in hand, he turned back the way he'd come.

"Teddy!" Katricia bellowed, getting off the bed as he started for the door again. "Dammit will you—"

The words died in her throat as he suddenly changed direction, heading for her instead of the door. He stopped in front of her, caught her upper arms, and pulled her up on her toes for a quick but very hard and thorough kiss. Then smiled wryly as he released her. "Sorry. Forgot. I won't be long."

Katricia blinked and simply stared as he turned and hurried out of the room. The stupid man thought she'd wanted a kiss good-bye. Which she would have wanted had he been going anywhere, but he wasn't going anywhere. She had no doubt he would realize that as soon as he ran into Bricker and Anders, but sighed and moved to the closet to retrieve her robe and don it before following him out of the room just in case the guys were still sleeping.

The house was silent as she moved out into the hall, and Katricia could see the door to the room at the far end of the hall was open, revealing a stripped bed. The door next to it was open as well, but didn't face in her direction. Still, she didn't doubt that bed would be stripped, too. Bricker and Anders were up and would stop Teddy, she thought with relief but continued on anyway.

The setup here was similar to Teddy's cottage, but bigger and arranged the opposite way. She stepped out of the hall into a large room with the right side an open living area separated from the kitchen and dining room on the left by a long counter. Her eyes landed on the twinkling lights of a large Christmas tree in front of the windows on the living-room side, and she stared at it for a moment, a slow smile spreading her lips. Bricker and Anders must have set it up. It hadn't been there before. They hadn't done a half-bad job decorating it, Katricia decided and then glanced toward the kitchen, spotting Teddy at once. He stood in front of the refrigerator, reading a note stuck to the metal front of it with a magnet.

"What does it say?" she asked, moving around the counter to join him.

"Woke early and decided to head back to T.O. Hoping to make it in time for Christmas dinner with Mortimer, Sam, and her sisters. Little elves peeled potatoes and turnip, stuffed the turkey, and popped it in the oven for you. Merry Christmas, your favorite elves J.B. and A.," Teddy read with bewilderment and then glanced to the stove and muttered, "I can smell the turkey. It must be nearly done."

He moved over to open the oven door and frowned when he saw the browning bird inside. The smell was heavenly, to Katricia's mind, but it just made Teddy frown harder. Slamming the door closed, he straightened. "Where did the turkey come from? And why the hell would they put it on a day early?"

"The blood courier brought the turkey and a bunch of other food," Katricia explained. "He had a trailer on the back of the snowmobile with that, the gas, the blood, and another snowmobile for us to use. But Bricker and Anders brought desserts and more food with the extra blood they brought up."

"Well, that was nice," he said grudgingly, and then asked with irritation, "But why the hell would they put it on today?"

"Because today is Christmas," she said gently, and when he glanced to her with horror, Katricia sighed and moved to slip her arms around his waist, explaining, "You were out for more than twenty-four hours, Teddy. It's Christmas Day. Well . . ." She smiled wryly as her gaze slid to the windows that made up the front wall of the cottage and she saw the darkness outside. "It's Christmas night now, I guess."

"Damn." Teddy sighed and slid his arms around her, his chin coming to rest on the top of her head. He hugged her tightly and then simply held her and muttered, "I'm sorry."

"For what?" she asked, pulling back to peer at him with surprise.

"I don't have a Christmas gift for you, or a birthday gift," he said sadly, and then shifted with frustration and muttered, "You've given me so much, I wanted to—"

"It's okay. I don't have anything for you, either," Katricia said soothingly.

Teddy stopped and peered at her with surprise. Then he snorted with disbelief. "You're kidding, right? Sweetheart, you've given me everything. You saved my life and much much more. You've given me a body that's young and healthy with not a single old-age ache or pain. And you've given me a smart, sexy woman for the rest of my days, not to mention a second chance at life."

"A second chance at life?" she echoed with surprise.

"I never married or had kids as a mortal, Katricia. Now I can. With you," he pointed out and then smiled crookedly and added, "And there won't be any more charity Christmases. I'll be spending them with you and our child when we have one."

She had no idea what a charity Christmas was, but was distracted by the other thing he'd said. "Our child."

"Yes . . . well, if you want kids," Teddy said uncertainly. "I do, but if you don't, we can—"

"I do," Katricia interrupted quickly and smiled when Teddy relaxed and grinned. She did want children. It just hadn't occurred to her until he'd mentioned them. She'd been too busy marveling over having a life mate to have moved on to the children part. But she did want them. Just maybe not for twenty years or so. Katricia figured in twenty years she should be used to having a life mate and not be trying to drag him off to the bedroom every five minutes. Maybe. She was certainly fighting the urge to do so now.

"I wish I had a gift for you. A whole passel of them for your birthday and Christmas both."

That fretful mutter from Teddy drew her attention to his unhappy expression, and she tightened her arms around him briefly.

"Teddy, you are a gift," she said solemnly. "I've been alive a long time and was starting to suffer the dark thoughts and depression that often lead to going rogue. But that's all gone now that I've found you." She leaned back and smiled. "You're a life mate. That's the gift every immortal prays they'll find under their tree at Christmas."

He peered at her silently for a moment and then his gaze slid past her and his eyes began to glow. Still looking past her, he asked, "With or without a bow?"

"What?" she asked with confusion and then gasped when he scooped her up into his arms.

"Did you want your life mate under that tree with or without a bow?" he asked, carrying her around the kitchen counter into the living-room area.

"Without," Katricia said with a laugh as she saw he was carrying her toward the Christmas tree. He set her on her feet once they reached the tree and immediately undid her robe, but when he reached for the lapels to remove it, she stopped him by clasping his face in both hands. When he raised his eyebrows and met her gaze in question, Katricia said solemnly, "You really are a gift, Teddy Brunswick. The best gift of all, one that promises many, many Merry Christmases and Happy Birthdays to come."

"For both of us," he vowed, and then bent his head to kiss her as his hands pushed the robe off her shoulders.

Home for the Holidays
by Jeaniene Frost

One

I glanced at my watch. Ten minutes to midnight. The vampire would be back soon, and despite hours of careful preparation, I wasn't ready for him.

A ghost's head popped through the wall, the rest of his body concealed by the wood barrier. He took one look around the room and a frown appeared on his filmy visage.

"You're not going to make it."

I yanked the wire through the hole I'd drilled into the ceiling's rafter, careful not to shift my weight too far or I'd fall off the ladder I was balanced on. Fabian was right, but I wasn't ready to concede defeat.

"When he pulls up, stall him."

"How am I supposed to do that?" he asked.

Good question. Unlike humans, vampires could see ghosts, but tended to ignore them as a general rule. While this vampire showed more respect to the corporeal-impaired, he still wouldn't stop to have a lengthy chat with one before entering his home.

"Can't you improvise? You know, make some loud pounding noises or cause the outer walls to bleed?"

The ghost shot me a look that said my witticism wasn't appreciated. "You watch too many movies, Cat."

Then Fabian vanished from sight, but not before I heard him muttering about unfair stereotypes.

I finished twisting together the wires along the ceiling. If all went well, as soon as the vampire came through that door, I'd use my remote transmitter to unload a surprise onto his head. Now, to set up the last of the contraptions I'd planned—

The unmistakable sound of a car approaching almost startled me into falling off the ladder. Damn it, the vampire was back! No time to rig any other devices. I barely had enough time to conceal myself.

I leapt off the ladder and carried it as noiselessly as I could to the closet. The last thing I needed was a bunch of metallic clanging to announce that something un- usual was going on. Then I swept up the silver knives I'd left on the floor. It wouldn't do for the vampire to see those right off.

I'd just crouched behind one of the living-room chairs when I heard a car door shut and then Fabian's voice.

"You won't believe what I found around the edge of your property," the ghost announced. "A cave with prehistoric paintings inside it!"

I rolled my eyes. *That* was the best tactic Fabian could come up with? This was a vampire he was trying to stall. Not a paleontologist.

"Good on you," an English voice replied, sounding utterly disinterested. Booted footsteps came to the door, but then paused before going further. I sucked in a breath I no longer needed. No cars were in the driveway, but did the vampire sense that several people lurked out of sight, waiting to pounce on him as soon as he crossed that threshold?

"Fabian," that cultured voice said next. "Are you sure there isn't anything *else* you want to tell me?"

A hint of menace colored the vampire's tone. I could almost picture my friend quailing, but his reply was instant.

"No. Nothing else."

"All right," the vampire said after a pause. The knob turned. "Your exorcism if you're lying."

I stayed hidden behind the chair, a silver knife gripped in one hand and the remote transmitter in the other. When the sound of boots hit the wood floor inside the house, I pressed the button and leapt up at the same time.

"Surprise!"

Confetti unleashed from the ceiling onto the vampire's head. With a whiplike motion, I threw my knife and severed the ribbon holding closed a bag of balloons above him. Those floated down more slowly, and by the time the first one hit the floor, the vampires who'd been concealed in the other rooms had come out.

"Happy birthday," they called out in unison.

"It's not every day someone turns two hundred and forty-five," I added, kicking balloons aside as I made my way to the vampire in the doorway.

A slow smile spread across his features, changing them from gorgeous to heart-stopping. Of course, my heart had stopped beating—for the most part—over a year ago, so that was my normal condition.

"This is what you've been so secretive about lately?" Bones murmured, pulling me into his arms once I got close.

I brushed a dark curl from his ear. "They're not just here for your birthday, they're staying for the holidays, too. We're going to have a normal, old-fashioned Christmas for once. Oh, and don't exorcise Fabian; I made him try to stall you. If you were ten minutes later, I'd have had streamers set up, too."

His chuckle preceded the brush of lips against my cheek; a cool, teasing stroke that made me lean closer in instinctive need for more.

"Quite all right. I'm sure I'll find a use for them."

Knowing my husband, he'd find several uses for them, and at least one of those would make me blush.

I moved aside to let Bones get enveloped in well-wishes from our guests. In addition to Fabian and his equally transparent girlfriend floating above the room, Bones's best friend, Spade, was here. So was Ian, the vampire who sired Bones; Mencheres, his young-looking vampire version of a grandfather; his girlfriend, Kira; and my best friend, Denise. She was the only one in the room with a heartbeat, making her seem human to anyone who didn't know better. Our guest list was small, because inviting everyone Bones knew for an extended birthday/holiday bash would require me renting a football stadium. Therefore, only Bones's closest companions were present.

Well, all except one.

"Anybody heard from Annette?" I whispered to Denise when she left Bones's side and returned to mine.

She shook her head. "Spade tried her twenty minutes ago, but she didn't answer her cell."

"Wonder what's keeping her."

Annette might not be my favorite person, considering her previous, centuries-long "friends with benefits" relationship with Bones, but she'd be last on the list of people I'd expect to skip his birthday party. Her ties with Bones went all the way back to when both of them were human, and in fairness, Annette seemed to have accepted that her position in his life was now firmly in the "friends *without* benefits" category.

"She flew in from London to be here," Denise noted. "Seems odd that she'd decide a thirty-minute car commute was too much."

"What's this?" Bones asked, making his way over.

I waved a hand, not wanting to spoil the festive mood. "Nothing. Annette must be running behind."

"Some bloke rang her right before we left the hotel. She said she'd catch up with us," Spade said, coming to stand behind Denise. With his great height, her head was barely even with his shoulders, but neither of them seemed to mind. Black hair spilled across his face as he leaned down to kiss her neck.

"Why am I the only one without someone to snog?" Ian muttered, giving me an accusatory glance. "Knew I should've brought a date."

"You didn't get to bring a date because the type of girl you'd pick would want to liven things up with a group orgy before cutting the cake," I pointed out.

His smile was shameless. "Exactly."

I rolled my eyes. "Deal with not being the center of slutty attention for once, Ian. It'll do you good."

"No it won't," he said, shuddering as if in horror. "Think I'll go to the hotel and see what's taking Annette."

Denise snorted. "Way to make do with who's available."

I bit back my laugh with difficulty. Denise's opinion of Ian—and Annette—was even worse than my own, but that didn't make her wrong. Still, out of respect for both of them being Bones's friends, I contained my snicker.

Far from being offended, Ian archly rose his brows. "Just following the American adage about turning a frown upside-down."

Mencheres, ever the tactful one, chose that moment to glide over. "Perhaps we should turn our attention to gifts."

Bones clapped Ian on the back. "Don't take too long, mate."

"I'll try to limit myself to an hour," Ian replied with a straight face.

"Pig," I couldn't help but mutter. Hey, I'd tried to rein myself in! If vampires could still get diseases, I'd wish a festering case of herpes on him, but I suppose it was a good thing that Ian's ability to carry or transmit STDs died with his humanity.

Ian left, chuckling to himself the whole time.

Bones's arm slid across my shoulders, his fingers stroking my flesh along the way. I'd worn a backless halter dress, because I knew he wouldn't be able to resist that bare expanse of skin, and I was right. Heat spilled over my emotions in its own caress as Bones dropped his shields so I could access his feelings. The tie that existed between us wasn't only forged in love. It was also the blood-deep, eternal link between a vampire and their sire. Bones had changed me from a half-vampire into a mostly-full one, and ever since, I could tap into his emotions like they were an extension of my own. There had been some serious drawbacks to my changing over, but I'd do it again just to have that level of intimacy between us.

Of course, that wasn't the only undead perk. The ability to heal instantly, fly, and mesmerize people didn't suck, either.

"Do you know how lovely you look?" he asked, his voice deepening in timber. Hints of glowing green appeared in his dark brown eyes, a visual cue of his appreciation.

I leaned in to whisper my reply. "Tell me later, when everyone's gone."

His laugh was low and promising. "That I will, Kitten."

We went into the next room, where a pile of presents awaited. Vampires had been called many things, but "stingy" usually wasn't among them. Bones had barely made a dent in opening his gifts before his cell phone rang. He glanced at the number with a chuckle.

"Ian, don't tell me you and Annette are too occupied to return," he said in lieu of a hello.

Supernatural hearing meant that I picked up every word of Ian's clipped reply.

"You need to get over here. Now."

Two

B ones and I were the only ones to enter the resort. The rest of our group stayed in the parking lot, keeping watch to make sure events didn't go from bad to worse with an ambush. Most people at the inn were sleeping this time of night, which I was grateful for. No intrusive chatter barraging my mind thanks to my unwanted ability to overhear humans' thoughts. Just the softer hum from dreams, which was as easy to tune out as your average background noise.

Once I followed Bones inside the Appalachian suite Annette had rented, however, the tranquil atmosphere shattered. Crimson streaked the walls, wood floors, and, in heavier quantities, the mattress. From the scent, it was Annette's blood, not someone else's. I expected the room to show signs of a fierce struggle, but not a stick of furniture seemed out of place.

Ian stood in the far corner of the room, his normally mocking countenance drawn into harsh lines of anger.

"In there," he said, jerking his head at the closed bathroom door.

Bones reached it in three long strides, but I hesitated. Ian hadn't told us if Annette was alive, just said to get here immediately. If Annette's body waited on the other side of that door, maybe I should give Bones a minute alone. She was the first vampire he'd ever made; her death would hit him hard. But even as I braced myself to comfort him, I heard a feminine, chiding voice.

"Really, Crispin, you shouldn't have come. You're missing your own party."

My brows shot up. Aside from calling Bones by his human name, which only a handful of people did, those upper-crust British tones identified the speaker as Annette. So much for her being dead. Hell, she didn't even sound fazed, as if her blood wasn't decorating the room in enough quantities to make it look like the inside of a slaughterhouse.

"I'm missing my own party? Have you lost your wits?" Bones asked her, echoing my own thoughts.

The door opened and Annette appeared. She wore only a robe, her strawberry-blond hair wet from what I guessed was a recent shower. This was one of the rare occasions I'd seen her without her face perfectly made up or her hair styled to the nines, and it made her look more vulnerable. Less like the undead bombshell who'd tried to scare me off when we first met, and more like a woman who seemed on the verge of tears despite her unfaltering smile.

"What a state this room is in," she said, letting out an embarrassed little laugh.

"Annette." Bones grasped her shoulders and forced her to look at him. "Who hurt you?"

Her hands fluttered on his arms, as if she wanted to push him away but didn't dare. "I don't know. I've never seen him before."

Bones studied the room, no doubt picking up nuances that even my battle-practiced gaze had missed. Two hundred years as an undead hit man made him formidable when it came to noticing incriminating details. Annette remained silent, the faint lines on her face deeper from her frown.

"You're lying," Bones finally said. "No forced entry on the doors, no signs of jimmying, so you let him in. Then you didn't struggle when he cut you, didn't wake the other guests with cries for help, and didn't call me though your bloody fingerprints are on your mobile. Ian, did you see who it was?"

"No, but I think I scared the sod off," Ian replied. "The window was open, and I heard something too fast to be human dashing away from the balcony, but I stayed with her instead of giving chase."

That surprised me. Ian loved few things more than a nasty brawl. Annette must be one of the few people he cared about, for him to be responsible by protecting her and calling for backup instead of indulging in a murderous game of hide-and-seek.

Though undead healing abilities meant there wasn't a scratch on her now, sometime after the others left to come to my house, at least one vampire had shown up and tortured the hell out of Annette. What made no sense was why she wouldn't tell us who it was, if Bones was right and she knew. Aside from the scent of blood, a harsh aroma hung in the room, a pungent combination of chemicals that seared my nose when I took in a breath. No use trying to determine her attacker by scent.

Annette remained silent. Bones's tone hardened.

"An attack against a member of my line is the same as an attack against me, so I'm no longer asking you as your friend. I'm commanding you as your sire to tell me *who did this*."

With those last three words, Bones unleashed his aura, and the weight of his power filled the room. This wasn't the tingling caress of sensations I'd felt from him earlier, but chilling waves of building pressure and crackling currents, like being in the center of an ice storm. Anyone undead within a hundred-yard radius would feel the force of Bones's aura, but most especially those tied to him through blood, as Annette and I were. She flinched as though he'd struck her, her champagne-colored gaze flickering between Bones and the floor.

"Crispin, I . . . I can't," she said at last, bowing her head. "I told you, I don't know."

Anger pulsed in palpable waves from Bones, showing that he didn't believe her. I was torn. Aside from one incident with me when we first met, Annette was as loyal to Bones as the day was long. She was still in love with him, too, and probably always would be. So why would she defy him over someone who'd tortured her? That was beyond my comprehension.

Unless she thought she was protecting Bones by her actions? I'd thrown myself in front of a few metaphorical trains for that reason. If Bones was right and Annette did know her attacker, maybe she thought whoever sliced and diced her was too powerful for Bones to take on in retaliation.

"Let's get her back to the house," I said, placing my hand on his arm to soothe away some of that furious energy. "We can figure out our next move there."

Bones gave Annette a look that promised he wasn't done with this discussion, but he swept his hand toward the door.

"All right, Kitten. After you."

Three

To give us some privacy, Spade, Denise, Mencheres, and Kira went back to the guest cabin instead of rejoining us at our home. We hadn't needed to update everyone on what happened. With their hearing, they'd gotten the full scoop while guarding the perimeter of the inn. Annette, Ian, Bones, and I filed back into my house, where the balloons, confetti, and banners now seemed out of place with our new, somber moods.

"Look at all these lovely gifts," Annette remarked.

"All I want to hear from you is a name," Bones cut her off. "Stop acting as though nothing happened and give it to me."

Annette flounced onto the couch with none of her usual grace. "I told you. I've never seen him before."

Bones sat on the couch across from her, stretching out his legs as though getting ready for an extended nap. "If that were true, you would have given me his description straightaway instead of trying to convince me that you don't know who he is."

"Not to mention you wouldn't have let him in, and you would've fought instead of lying quiet while he carved into you," Ian added, ignoring the dirty look Annette shot him.

Both men had very good points.

"You're wasting your time hoping Bones will let this go," I chimed in. "No self-respecting Master would allow the torture of one of his people to go unpunished. *You* told me that yourself a long time ago."

Under these admonitions, Annette should have folded. Everything we'd said was true, and she knew it. Yet when I saw her lips compress together, I could tell she still wouldn't budge even though it made no sense.

Fabian materialized in the center of the room. "There's a vampire in the woods!"

I immediately jumped to my feet, going to our nearest cache of weapons. Ian didn't seem interested in armoring up first. He started toward the door.

"Stop."

The single word came from Bones. He hadn't moved from his position on the couch, his lean body still sprawled as if totally relaxed. I knew better. The tension exuding from his aura made the air feel thicker.

"I hoped we'd be followed here," Bones went on in that same quiet, unyielding voice. "Now we don't need Annette to tell us who her attacker was. We'll find out for ourselves."

"Crispin, wait," Annette began, alarm crossing her features.

"You had your chance," he said shortly. Then he glanced at Ian and nodded in Annette's direction. Whatever else she was about to say was cut off when Ian slapped his hand over her mouth. Only faint, muffled grunts came from her as Ian settled on the couch behind Annette, dragging her tight up against him.

"Don't fret. She'll stay quiet like a good girl, won't you, poppet?" Ian drawled in her ear.

Annette's grunts now sounded furious, but there was no way she could overpower Ian. That was also why I wasn't too worried about our uninvited guest. Either he was suicidal, or he had no idea that he was sneaking up a hill where there were several Master vampires, one of whom could rip his head off with merely his thoughts.

"Fabian, you only saw one vampire?"

The ghost bobbed his head. "On the lower half of the hill."

Must be why the others didn't sense him yet. Our house and guesthouse were on the highest point of this hill, deliberately less accessible to any passersby.

"Kitten, come with me," Bones said, rising at last. "Fabian, tell the others to stay inside and talk as though nothing's amiss."

I finished strapping more silver knives to the sheaths lining my arms. Wooden stakes would've been cheaper, but those only worked in the movies. Then I threw a coat on, not for warmth against the frigid November evening but to conceal all my weapons.

"Ready," I said, my fangs popping out of their own accord.

Ian snorted. "Appears as if Christmas has come early for you, Cat."

I glowered at him, but the exhilaration coursing through me must be evident from my aura. I hadn't wanted a knife-happy intruder to crash Bones's birthday party, but it had been weeks since I'd indulged in a little ass-kicking. Who could blame me for wanting to show this vampire what happened to anyone coming around my house looking for trouble?

"Remember we need him alive, luv," Bones said. His gaze flared emerald with his own form of predatory anticipation. "For now at least."

Frost-coated leaves crunched underneath my feet as I walked through the woods. My strappy heeled sandals were the worst choice of footwear for any normal person navigating these steep hills, but vampires had great reflexes and couldn't catch cold, so I hadn't bothered to change my shoes. Plus, if it made me look more vulnerable to whoever was prowling out here in the dark with me, so much the better.

Bones was somewhere flying above, but I didn't see him, due to his clothing blending against the night sky, or him being too high up. I didn't see Fabian or his ghostly girlfriend, either, but I knew they were out here, ready to notify our friends if our prowler turned out to have an entourage. We'd guarded the location of our Blue Ridge home from all but close friends and family, yet if one enemy had found us, others might have, too.

Twigs snapped about a hundred yards to my left. I didn't jerk my head in that direction, but continued on my way as if I were out for a leisurely midnight stroll. I doubted our trespasser would fall for the act, but he had to be somewhat stupid or he wouldn't have attacked Annette while Bones was within striking distance. No Master vampire worth their fangs would stand for that.

More crackling noises sounded, too close for me to pretend not to hear them anymore. I turned in that direction, widening my eyes as if I hadn't already noticed the shadowy figure lurking behind the trees.

"Is someone there?" I called out, edging my tone with worry.

Laughter rolled across the cold night air. "You'd make a terrible horror-movie heroine. You neglected to hunch your shoulders, clutch your coat, and bite your bottom lip ever so tremulously."

His accent was English, and his manner of speaking sounded more like Spade and Annette's aristocratic dialect than Bones and Ian's less formal vernacular. Shoulder-length blond hair caught the moonlight as he stepped out from behind the trees.

It wasn't his looks that made me stare, though the vampire's chiseled cheekbones and finely sculpted features reminded me of Bones's flawless beauty. Or his height, and he had to be at least six two. It was his shirt. Lace spilled out from under his coat sleeves to almost cover his hands. More of that frothy white stuff gathered at his neck and hung midway down his chest. I almost forgot to scan him for weapons, it was so distracting.

"Are you serious?" I couldn't help but blurt. "Because RuPaul would think twice before wearing that in public."

His smile showed white teeth without any hint of fang. "A nod to my heritage. I drew the line at the tights, though, as you can see."

He wore black jeans, so yes, far more modern than his top. The jeans also showed off the silver knife strapped to the vampire's thigh, but aside from a long wooden walking stick, that was the only visible weapon he carried. Didn't mean it was the only weapon he had; all my best stuff was hidden, too.

"Let me guess. You're lost?"

I started to close the distance between us. Although he didn't have a speck of blood on him, chances were I was looking at Annette's attacker. His aura marked him as a couple hundred years old, but I wasn't afraid. Unless he was cloaking his power, he wasn't a Master, which meant I could wipe the floor with him.

The vampire appraised me in the same way I looked him over; thorough, assessing, and unafraid. All the while, that little smirk never left his face.

"Beautiful, aren't you, though I don't care for the short hair. You'd look lovelier with long, flowing red locks."

Something about him seemed familiar, even though I was sure we'd never met. His cockiness would certainly make him memorable.

"Yeah, well, I got my hair styled by inferno three weeks ago, so it's still growing back," I said flippantly.

If I wasn't a vampire, I wouldn't have hair at all after being nearly burned to death, but undead regenerative abilities meant I didn't need to invest in wigs. Or skin grafts, thank God.

"So, you want to talk more?" I went on. "Or should I just start whipping your ass for trespassing and probable assault?"

I was now close enough that I could see his eyes were the color of blueberries, but he didn't react in anger. Instead, his grin widened.

"If you weren't my relation, I'd be tempted to take you up on your flirting."

The idiot thought I was hitting on him? That annoyed me into missing the first part of his sentence, but then I froze.

"What do you mean, relation?"

The only family I had aboveground consisted of an imprisoned vampire father, a ghostly uncle, and a newly-undead mother. Yet the conviction in his tone and the steady way he held my gaze had me wondering if he was telling the truth. Good Lord, was it possible that my father wasn't the only vampire in my family ancestry?

He traced a line in the dry leaves with that long stick, his brow arching in challenge.

"Haven't figured it out yet?" He gave a mock sigh. "Thought out of everyone, you'd be most attuned to the similarities, but appears not."

Word games weren't the right move with me. I gave his long blond locks and intentionally outdated shirt a withering glance. "If you're trying to double as Lestat, then sure, you nailed it with the similarities."

He snorted. "Thick little kitten, aren't you?"

Something dark dropped down behind him, but before the vampire could whirl around to defend himself, he was enveloped in a punishing embrace. Moonlight glinted off the blade Bones held to the vampire's chest.

"No one calls my wife that but me," he said in a deadly, silken voice.

The vampire twisted in a futile attempt to free himself, but iron bars would've been easier to pry off. His thrashing drove the tip of Bones's knife into his chest, darkening that white lacy shirt with crimson. More struggling would only shove the blade deeper, and if that silver twisted in his heart, the vampire would be dead the permanent way. He stilled, craning his neck to peer back at the man restraining him.

In that moment, seeing their faces so close together, the first inkling of realization slammed into me. It seemed impossible, but. . .

"Bones, don't hurt him!" I said, reeling at the implications. "I— I think maybe this isn't about Annette's attack."

The vampire shot me an approving look. "Not so thick after all, are you?"

Bones didn't move the blade, but his hand tightened around the hilt of the knife. "Insult her again and those will be your last words."

A pained laugh came out of the vampire. "Here I thought teasing one's relation was normal."

"Relation?" Bones scoffed. "You're claiming to be a member of her family?"

"Not by blood, but by marriage," the vampire said, drawing each word out. "Allow me to introduce myself. My name is Wraith, and I'm your brother."

Four

Shock washed over Bones's face. Wraith seemed more urbane, even with a knife protruding from his chest.

"Lies," Bones finally said. "My mother had no other children aside from me."

"She didn't," was Wraith's reply. "Your father did."

Bones still looked thunderstruck, but his grip didn't loosen. "My mum was a whore. There's no way she could've known who my father was."

"Your mother was Penelope Ann Maynard, who did indeed become a whore. But not until *after* she bore the Duke of Rutland's illegitimate son. That son was raised in a London whorehouse and sentenced to deportation for thievery in 1789. He died in the New South Wales penal colonies a year later, but he didn't stay dead."

Wraith's gaze slid to the man behind him. "Any of this sound familiar to you?"

Each word hammered into Bones like physical blows, I could tell from the emotions weaving into my subconscious. While I'd heard the story of Bones's past, it wasn't common knowledge, and Wraith had been spot-on with the dates and details. Plus, there was the resemblance. Both men had those high, chiseled cheekbones, thick brows, full yet firm mouths, and tall, proudly arrogant stances. Bones was a brown-eyed brunet and Wraith a blue-eyed blond, but if Wraith dyed his hair and got dark contacts, even a casual observer could guess they were related. Half-brothers, if what Wraith said was true.

"Close, but my mother's surname was Russell, not Maynard," Bones stated. "And neither she nor any of the women I grew up with even hinted that they knew who my father was. Now, over two hundred years later, you expect me to believe this tale of dukes and you being my long-lost brother?" His arm tightened around Wraith's neck. "Sorry, mate. I don't."

"I . . . ave . . . oof." The words were garbled from the pressure Bones put on the vampire's throat.

"Proof?" Bones asked, loosening his grip.

Wraith managed a nod. "If you stop throttling me, I'll show you."

Fabian followed us at a discreet distance as we walked down the winding gravel road that led to the bottom of the hill. If Wraith noticed the ghost flitting above the tree tops, he didn't comment. In fact, he seemed relaxed. Cheerful even, but I didn't let down my guard. I'd had people smile the whole time they attempted to kill me, so a jolly disposition might indicate good intentions if you were Santa Claus, but the same didn't go for vampires.

"How did you find my house?" Bones asked. He also hadn't lost an inch of his wariness, as the currents swirling around him indicated.

"I followed you from the hotel," Wraith replied.

I stopped short. "You're admitting you're the asshole who carved up Annette?" Brother-in-law or not, he'd pay if he was.

Wraith sighed. "I *rescued* Annette by chasing that vampire off. Didn't catch him, though. By the time I returned to check on her, you were loading her into the car, and the lot of you looked angry enough to kill first and ask questions later."

Ian had said he'd heard a vampire when he first arrived. He'd thought it was the perpetrator fleeing the scene, but could it have been Wraith chasing after the real attacker?

"If that's true, why wouldn't Annette mention you when we arrived? And more importantly, where were you when some sod was painting the walls with her blood?"

Wraith cast a sideways glance at the flatness in Bones's tone. He wouldn't need to be linked to his emotions to know that Bones didn't believe this version of events.

"I was on my way to see her. You can check her mobile; the call she received right before she was attacked was me telling her I was running late. When I arrived, I heard something odd. Her door was unlocked, so I entered in time to see someone dash out the window. After checking that Annette was still alive, I chased him. As for why she didn't mention me, I can only guess it was due to a misguided attempt to keep the surprise."

"What surprise?" Bones and I asked in unison.

"That you have a brother," Wraith replied softly. "The news was to be Annette's birthday present to you."

Even with their similarity in appearance, it still seemed impossible to think that Wraith was Bones's brother. From the disbelief threading into my subconscious, Bones felt the same way.

"This vampire you chased, did you get a good look at him? Happen to recognize him?" I asked, changing the subject.

"Sorry, never seen him before. The only thing I can tell you is that he had dark hair and could fly like the wind."

A brunet vampire who could fly. That narrowed it down to at least ten thousand—not much help at all. We were almost at the bottom of the hill. Up ahead, a Buick was parked on the side of the road, its lights off.

"My car," Wraith said, nodding at it. Then he held out a set of keys. "The proof you seek is in the boot."

Bones didn't touch the keys, but a tight smile stretched his lips. "Don't think so. You open it."

Wraith snorted in a way that sounded very familiar. "Think I've wired it to explode? You're even more paranoid than your reputation."

"I'm also more impatient than my reputation," Bones replied coolly. "So get on with it."

With another noise of exasperation, Wraith set down his long stick and walked over to the back of the car. The trunk popped up without even a spark and Wraith pulled out a flat, sheet-draped, rectangular object.

"Here," he said, holding it out to Bones. "I also have archives, but if this doesn't convince you, those won't either."

Bones took it and pulled the sheet away. It was a painting; old, from the state of the framing and the canvas, but I didn't need more than a single glance at the subject to let out a gasp.

Bones said nothing, simply staring at the image of a man who bore an eerie resemblance to him, only his hair was corn-silk blond and he had lines around his mouth that looked too harsh to be caused by smiling. He wore a ruffled shirt and an embroidered coat with so many tassels, buttons, and braids that it looked like it could stand on its own. A jewel-handled dirk sticking out of his belt completed the image of extravagance, as if the arrogance in the man's expression wasn't clue enough that he'd been born to a life of luxury.

"Meet the Duke of Rutland," Wraith said, his voice breaking the heavy silence. "In case his face isn't proof enough, records show that he was christened Crispin Phillip Arthur Russell, the Second. My human name was Crispin Phillip Arthur Russell, the Third. Same as yours."

I flashed to eight years ago, when I was still getting to know Bones and he told me the reason behind his real name.

Merely a bit of fancy on my mum's part, since clearly she had no idea who my da was. Still, she thought adding numerals after my name would give

me a bit of dignity. Poor sweet woman, ever reluc-
tant to face reality . . .

If the vampire standing across from us was correct, Bones's mother hadn't called him "the third" on a whim. She'd named him after the father he never knew he had.

When Bones spoke, his voice was strained from the emotions I could feel him fighting to contain.

"If you're my half-brother, that makes you over two hundred years old. If you knew of our ties, why, in all that time, did you never attempt to find me before now?"

Wraith's smile was sad. "I didn't know until recently when I heard your real name from some war-mongering ghouls. I thought it was a jest, but then I found a picture of you. Our resemblance was enough to get me digging into my family history. In some very old archives, I found mention of a sum my father paid to Viscount Maynard for reparations concerning the viscount's unwed pregnant daughter, Penelope. Then your name appeared in the Old Bailey trial transcripts, and your age matched how old the child would've been. If that plus our identical names wasn't enough, meeting you is. You look and act enough like my father to be his dark-haired ghost."

Something else swirled amidst the wariness in Bones's emotions, something so poignant it brought tears to my eyes. *Hope.* Was it really possible that after all this time, Bones had found a living member of his family? Wraith's real name, resemblance, and the portrait were damn compelling, not to mention the records Wraith cited could be easily authenticated. Plus, why would someone go to the trouble of lying about a family connection? Bones wasn't the type of person who'd appreciate being Punk'd.

I linked my arm with his, hoping to help calm his whirling emotions. "You say Annette knew about this?"

Wraith nodded. "I thought news such as this should be delivered in person, so I went looking for a member of your line who'd know your location. Once Annette was satisfied of my claims, we agreed to meet at the hotel, intending to arrive here together."

"As my present," Bones murmured, looking over Wraith with more curiosity than suspicion this time.

A smile quirked Wraith's mouth. "Afraid I drew the line at tying a bow around myself."

The fictional detective Sherlock Holmes had said that once you eliminate the impossible, whatever was left, no matter how improbable, had to be the truth. It seemed unbelievable that the vampire standing across from us was Bones's brother, but so far the facts pointed to that very thing.

"I know this may be rather startling," Wraith went on, still with that same lopsided half-smile. "Or you might not care. So much time has passed since our humanity that I understand if this news means little to you. If you'd rather I leave, I will, but I— I had hoped that perhaps we could get to know one another."

If I hadn't been touching Bones, I wouldn't have noticed the slight tremor that went through him when Wraith stumbled over those last words, showing a glimpse of vulnerability underneath that cocky exterior. Wraith might claim he'd be okay, but it seemed clear that a rebuff would wound him. As for Bones, I could tell he very much wanted to know more about this vampire who might be the only link to his long-lost human family.

A gust of frigid wind blew Wraith's hair around his face, reminding me that we could continue this conversation in comfort instead of standing along the side of a road.

I smiled at him. "Why don't we go back to the house? It's warmer there, and then I can congratulate Annette on her choice of a gift. She topped my present by a mile."

Five

W raith's eyes widened when we walked into the cabin and he saw Annette being restrained by Ian, the other vampire's hand still clamped over her mouth.

"Oh, don't worry about that. We had, uh, a prior failure to communicate," I said by way of explanation.

Ian's brows rose but he didn't let go of Annette. "If this is our trespasser, care to explain why he's not in pieces?"

"He's not the bloke who butchered Annette," Bones said, clearing his throat. "Turns out, he might be my . . . my brother."

Bones reiterated Wraith's story, uncovering the painting for illustration. Ian looked stunned at the revelation of both Bones's parents being members of the nobility, but Bones didn't notice. His attention was all for the blond vampire standing beside him.

"Hmmph," was what Ian said when Bones was finished. "So your human father was the Duke of Rutland, but who was your vampire sire, Wraith?"

"His name was Sheol, but he's been dead for over a century," Wraith replied.

I made appropriate sympathetic noises, but in truth, I was relieved. How awkward would it have been if Wraith was part of an enemy's line? To say vampires existed under a feudalistic system was to put it nicely. It could be better compared to the way the Mafia operated. On steroids.

"How tragic." Ian didn't even try to sound sympathetic, but that was par for the course with him. "Whose protection have you been under since then?"

Wraith squared his shoulders. "I've stayed Masterless."

"At your power level?" Open disbelief colored Ian's words.

My jaw dropped. I'd also noticed that Wraith's aura didn't mark him as particularly strong, but it was crossing a line to rub that in.

Bones agreed. "Ian," he drew out in warning.

"Quite all right," Wraith said, but his lips had thinned to twin slits. "I kept to myself most of the time. Might be lonely that way, but safer considering the many power struggles our kind indulges in."

Annette elbowed Ian in the ribs. At that, he finally took his hand off her mouth.

"I'm so pleased you made it here, Wraith," she said. Her gaze slid to Bones. "It's not how I imagined the two of you would meet, of course . . ."

Wraith came forward to take her hand, kissing it. "You couldn't help that terrible attack. I'm only relieved that I arrived when I did. I vow I'll find whoever did it and repay him in kind."

Annette didn't refute a word, indicating that Wraith had told the truth about his actions at the inn. That meant we had another problem on our hands, but I was glad it didn't involve the tawny-haired vampire who seemed more and more likely to be Bones's brother.

Annette rose from the couch, her pale amber gaze meeting Bones's dark brown eyes.

"Crispin, I assure you that I checked into Wraith's claims when he first contacted me. I'd never have arranged to bring him here otherwise. From everything I discovered, he is exactly who he maintains himself to be—your half-brother."

"I'll turn the archives I mentioned over to you," Wraith added. "They're in my car. Modern technology could confirm it as well, if you wish to compare our DNA—"

"Excellent notion, I know a bloke who can run those tests," Ian interrupted.

"Stop," Bones said, holding out his hand. A smile twisted his mouth before he went on. "I'm sure tomorrow I'll want to see everything concerning your, or our, family history, but right now, I'd like to just . . . talk for a bit. Get to know one another."

Wraith stared at Bones, his expression mirroring the same cautious optimism I felt from Bones's emotions.

"I'd like that," he rasped.

Ian opened his mouth, but my hand landed on his shoulder. "Let's go tell the others about our new guest," I said, squeezing hard in warning. "Annette, why don't you come with us? We'll get your bags and you can put something else on."

Ian glared at me, but I only smiled sweetly while tightening my grip. He could be his normal dickish self some other time. Annette needed no persuading to give Bones a little privacy with Wraith. She almost snatched at Ian's hand to tug him away.

"Come along. If I have to wear this dreadful robe a moment longer, I'll stake myself."

Dawn was near by the time Bones slipped into bed. I'd come up a couple hours ago, not to sleep, but to just mull over the evening's surprising events. On one hand, I was thrilled at the prospect of Bones finding a member of his presumed dead family. On the other, my initial excitement over Wraith had become tempered by nagging questions. Maybe Ian's negativity was just rubbing off on me, but why hadn't Annette mentioned to anyone that, oh, by the way, she was bringing Bones's long lost *brother* with her tonight? It was one thing to surprise Bones with the news, another to drop that bomb on everyone else, too.

And why hadn't she mentioned Wraith when we arrived at the hotel? For God's sake, we could have accidentally killed him while looking for her attacker! When Ian asked Annette this question, she didn't have an answer, seeming a little baffled by her actions, too. I found it rather strange. Granted, I might have assigned a few uncharitable words to Annette over the years, but "airhead" wasn't usually one of them.

Then there was the tidbit Fabian revealed after I excused myself to go upstairs. In his hurry to tell us that an unfamiliar vampire prowled around our property, Fabian had neglected to mention what he saw him doing. According to Fabian, Wraith had been circling the lower part of the hill while periodically cutting his hand to sprinkle blood on the ground.

Even for a vampire, that was plain weird. Wraith's family ties to Bones so far seemed solid, but being family didn't automatically make someone honorable. I knew that better than most people. Still, I didn't want to immediately attack Bones with my doubts, so I rolled into his arms with only three words.

"How was it?"

Wraith was in one of our guest rooms below, but I wasn't worried about being overheard. Due to recent events, we'd modified our bedroom. It was now soundproofed as well as ghost-proofed, thanks to copious amounts of weed and garlic between the thick insulation in the walls. With that and our low voices, not even an attentive vampire could catch our conversation.

Bones ran his hands along the length of my back, causing me to scoot closer in enjoyment. He always came to bed naked, and the feel of his hard, sleek body was enough to make me want to skip talking altogether, but this was important.

"Pleasant, for the most part." Then he paused, seeming to choose his words. "Bluebloods often sired bastards in both the upper and lower classes, so I have fewer doubts about Wraith being my relation than I do about the type of man he is. The former, he seems eager to discuss. The latter, he's reticent about."

That mirrored my own concerns, but I'd let him go first. "How so?"

"His sire was killed, nothing unusual in that." Bones paused again, and I could almost feel his cynicism battling with his desire to believe Wraith. "Yet he continues to claim no real association with vampires since then. Even if he stayed out of political alliances for safety reasons, our kind isn't known to be solitary."

"Maybe he doesn't want to admit he's pals with some of your enemies because he's worried it'll affect your opinion of him?" I had my doubts about this, but for Bones's sake I'd suggest an optimistic reason.

"Perhaps," he mused. "What do you make of him?"

"With the resemblance, name, documents, and portrait being so easy to authenticate, I think he's probably your brother, but that doesn't mean I trust him," I said honestly, and proceeded to outline my concerns.

His expression tightened as I spoke. By the time I was finished, he let out a sigh.

"Nothing to do but investigate him, then. If he can't accept my doing that, then we've no hope of a relationship. I wouldn't fault him for looking into my life before seeking me out. Two centuries is too long to throw caution to the winds for sentiment, even if we are family."

"You're two hundred and forty-five," I reminded him, changing the subject. We both agreed that Wraith needed checking out, plus we had to hunt for the vampire who attacked Annette, but we could do those things later. Right now, I wanted Bones focused on pleasant things, not more stresses. It was his birthday, after all.

I slid my thigh between his, brow arching in challenge. "So, you ready for your other present? Or now that you're almost a quarter-millennium old, maybe you want to take a nap instead?"

His laugh was sin at its most tempting. "For that, luv, I'll make you beg."

Bones rolled, yanking me on top of him. He gripped my wrists in one hand, the other urging up my short silk nightie. Unlike him, I never went to bed naked. Not when it was so arousing to let him peel the clothes from me.

"Let go of my hands," I said, aching to run them over his body and feel the myriad of muscles beneath his pale, smooth skin. Already his power flowed over me, vibrating along my nerve endings like seeking, invisible fingers.

He chuckled as he used his free hand to part my legs. "You forgot to say the magic word."

Then he slid down the bed, letting go of my wrists. I tried to move them, but found my wrists still held in an unbreakable grip, this time with invisible bands of power instead of flesh.

"I see you've been practicing with your new teleki-nesis," I said breathily. "That's cheating."

He laughed again as that flex of power kept me where I was. Strong fingers kneaded the small of my back as he pulled me closer, bringing my lower half to his mouth. I sucked in a gasp when his lips caressed my stomach, tongue teasing my navel with flickering strokes before continuing downward. His fangs snagged on the top of my panties, tugging them, but far too slowly. My strad-dling him hindered their removal, too, but when I tried to swing my leg around, he stopped me.

"Something you want?" he murmured.

His mouth was so close that his lips brushed against the lace underwear I now cursed myself for putting on.

"I want these off," I said, arching toward him. For a split second his mouth pressed to my flesh, shooting red-hot pleasure through me as his tongue snaked out with devastating skill. But then it was gone, leaving me throbbing with need.

"Bones, please," I moaned.

A dark laugh made everything flame where his breath landed. "You call that begging? Oh, Kitten, you can do much better than that . . ."

Six

I awoke to a vampire leaning over me, nothing un-usual since I'd gone to sleep wrapped in one's arms. But what made *this* out of the ordinary was that the vampire wasn't Bones.

Ian's hand clapped over my mouth before I could snap out an indignant demand for him to leave. I grabbed his arm, intending to break it in several places, when my sleep-fuzzy vision cleared enough to note the gravity in his expression.

"Shh," he whispered.

I nodded, torn between thinking he better have a damn good reason for this stunt and being afraid that he did. Ian removed his hand and I sat up, my gaze darting around. No one else was in the room, and he had the door closed.

"What's wrong?" I asked at once.

Ian kept his voice very low. "Crispin is acting strange."

"Crispin as in Bones, or Crispin as in Wraith?" We had two of them now, and Bones had seemed fine when I last saw him.

"The only Crispin I give a shite about," Ian snapped. "Really, we don't have time for these games."

I couldn't agree more, which was why I didn't appreciate Ian sneaking into my room and gagging me just to tell me he thought Bones was acting oddly. For God's sake, his heretofore unknown brother was in town and he'd resolved to investigate that brother for possible nefarious intentions. It would get under anyone's skin.

Still, in case Ian wasn't overreacting . . . "Strange how?"

"He's inordinately cheerful, and he seems almost oblivious to anyone but Wraith. Same with everyone else. I tell you, something is going on."

If I weren't naked, I would've shoved Ian out the door right then. "I knew you were shallow, but *really*? Bones just found out he has a brother and he's not sure what type of man that brother is. The rest of us aren't, either. So yes, for a little while, Wraith might get more attention than you. Man up and stop acting like a brat who hates the new baby because now Mommy and Daddy don't play with him as much!"

"This isn't about my shallowness," Ian said curtly. Then he strode to the door. "When you realize that, meet me at the Hampton Inn in Asheville, unless you've been affected, too."

"You're staying there?" Part of me was relieved. Now I didn't have to deal with him through the holidays.

"Yes," was his short reply. "Someone has to find out what rock Wraith crawled out from under."

He left then, shutting the door behind him. I heaved a sigh and got out of bed. *He's as shallow as a kiddie pool,* I told myself, but my own niggling seeds of doubt had made me speed through showering and getting dressed. Ian was egotistical, perverted, and morally bankrupt, but he wasn't prone to overreacting about anything except involuntary abstinence. *Could something be wrong with Bones?*

Right, because acting jovial while trying to glean facts out of his brother couldn't be a cross-examination tactic—it clearly spells menacing omen, an inner voice mocked.

That was the most logical explanation. Still, I couldn't squelch my unease as I headed downstairs. When you've seen bodies come back from the dead as attack zombies, you pretty much realize that anything is possible. Bones's laughter rang out loud and hearty, and though the sound normally gladdened me, thanks to Ian, it almost sounded foreboding now.

Nothing's wrong, nothing's wrong, I chanted to myself as I followed the sounds into the kitchen. Ian had apparently left, but the others were gathered at the table. Wraith sat at the head, his blond hair gathered in a ponytail that somehow looked masculine, and wearing another shirt that would be in line with Renaissance festival attire.

"Cat," he said, smiling at me. "Do have a seat."

Inviting me to sit at my own table. How kind. I squelched that sarcastic response and pulled up a chair from the other room, our kitchen table merely seating six. Only after I settled in did it occur to me that Bones hadn't offered to get the chair.

Granted, I wasn't the type of girl who waited for someone to open doors or slide out chairs for me, but Bones normally got a kick out of gestures like that. Furthermore, Spade and Mencheres were chivalrous almost to a pathological fault, but they hadn't spoken up, either. *It's nothing,* I told myself, and pasted a false smile on my face.

"So what did I miss?"

Wraith settled back more comfortably in his chair. "I was telling everyone about the time I absconded with the Duke of Rutland's prized stallion as a lad."

Five hours later, Wraith still hadn't shut up, and aside from me and Denise, no one else seemed to want him to. I'd found exciting activities like starting the dishwasher or doing a load of laundry to avoid Wraith's droning on, but aside from that and Denise's occasional trips to the bathroom, no one else moved except to relocate from the kitchen to the family room. Denise caught my eye a few times and raised her brows as if to ask, what's the deal?

Damned if I knew. It was one thing for Bones to lull Wraith into revealing information by pretending to be interested in his background. Not his usual interrogation technique—that normally involved knives and lots of screaming—but with their probable family ties, I'd buy the gentler approach. I'd even buy that the others were onto this strategy and backing Bones's play by also pretending to be engrossed by Wraith's tales.

But it was one thing to feign attentiveness and another to look almost spellbound. Hell, details of life as an eighteenth-century aristocrat should be boring to Spade and Annette. They'd both been wealthy members of Britain's peerage, too, so Wraith wasn't telling them anything they didn't know from experience.

Right after night fell, Denise came over, her smile too stiff to be genuine. "You mind going for a walk, Cat?"

"Sure. Be back, everyone, we'll round up some firewood while we're out," I said, raising my voice though that shouldn't have been necessary.

No one even glanced up. Okay, the chair thing could've been overlooked, but three normally gallant men not commenting about two chicks gathering *firewood* in the dark? That was downright uncharacteristic, even if I could see at night.

Fabian gave me a helpless look, swishing around the ceiling in nervous circles. I jerked my head toward the door and he zoomed outside without further prompting. Again, no one seemed to notice. They all kept staring at Wraith like he'd hung the moon, and here he was talking about the most boring-sounding ball ever.

"Guess the honeymoon's over," Denise muttered once we were outside. "Next I suppose I'll be sleeping in the wet spot."

I walked past the stacked logs on the side of the house and kept heading into the woods. Fabian followed behind us, flitting through the trees instead of around them. No one from the house appeared to be paying attention to us, but just in case, I wanted to be far enough away that we wouldn't be overheard.

"I mean, I get that it's a huge deal that Bones's long-lost brother showed up," Denise went on. "I'm happy for him, and I'm not trying to steal Wraith's thunder.

But Spade could give me a grunt every couple hours, you know?"

I kept walking at a brisk pace. With Denise's demonically-altered stamina, she was able to keep up with ease. When we were halfway down the hill, I finally spoke.

"I can't believe I'm saying this, but . . . Ian was right. Something strange *is* going on."

Denise stopped, her hazel eyes widening. "Ian said that? Thank God I'm not the only one thinking it!"

"Keep your voice down," I reminded her, adding, "It's got to be Wraith. Everyone is acting, well, kinda mesmerized by him, except vampires can't mesmerize other vampires."

"True. Besides, we're not affected," Denise pointed out.

"Neither is Ian."

Fabian and his girlfriend, Elisabeth, also weren't, but ghosts were normally immune to anything that affected the living or the undead. I suppose I still could have some of that same immunity in my system due to my recently absorbing a voodoo queen's powers over the other side; my unprecedented status as a vampire who fed off of and absorbed powers from undead blood had thrown a monkey wrench into things before. But if Wraith had some sort of unknown snake-charmer mojo, then Denise and Ian should also be gathered around him in rapt attention. Not wondering, like me, about what was going on.

I waved the ghost over. "Fabian, what do you think?"

"I suspect magic," he replied. "I searched Wraith's room and found a bloody symbol drawn on the floor under a rug. Why would he do that and hide it, unless he had ill intentions?"

We were in agreement about that, but I wanted to be absolutely sure we weren't overreacting before I started conspiring with Ian. Maybe Wraith was just superstitious.

"I'm going back there and pulling Bones aside. Find out right now if this is all an act or not."

Denise touched my arm. "Be careful, Cat. If Wraith has . . . I don't know, bewitched everyone, then you'll tip your hand that you're onto him."

I sighed. "Fine, I'll be subtle. After I talk to Bones, if I say that I can't find my boots, you'll know it's not an act, so you'll need to play *Stepford Wives* along with everyone else."

"And what will you do then?" Fabian asked.

I smiled with a touch of grimness. "I'll meet Ian in Asheville, and we'll find a way to stop Wraith."

Seven

The six of them were still in their same spots in the family room when we came back inside. Denise went straight upstairs, but I pasted on my best hostess smile as I walked over to Bones, laying my hand on his shoulder.

"Pardon me, but I need to steal my husband away for a few minutes."

It took two tugs on his shoulder, but he finally glanced up. "Why?"

I kept my smile even though the question was curt. "Because, *dear*, I need your help with something."

"Whatever it is, I'm sure you can manage."

Ice raced up my spine. His expression was cold, and the look he gave me was the one I'd seen him bestow on enemies before a brawl that ended bloody. Never had I thought to be on the receiving end of such a glare from Bones, and the fact that it was over something so small made my sense of foreboding triple.

This wasn't just odd behavior. It was as if Bones had been replaced with a stranger.

I met Wraith's gaze, noting the surprise that flickered over his face before he covered it with a smile.

"I've monopolized everyone too long, I fear. I'll retire to my room for a bit."

Several instant protests met this statement, until Wraith held out his hands.

"Please, everyone. Attend to your lovely ladies. I'll see you later."

As if a switch had been flipped, Bones turned to me and smiled, his expression warm. "What did you need?"

I kept my jaw from swinging, with the utmost difficulty. "It's in our room," I managed. "Come with me."

My rising fears made the steps leading there feel like they'd morphed into miles. By the time we crossed the threshold, I was almost vibrating with agitation.

"What the fuck is going on?" I demanded as soon as I shut the door. So much for subtlety.

Bones frowned. "Blimey, what's gotten into you that you're in such a lather?"

"What's gotten into me? *Me?*" I repeated, catching myself before I became more shrill. Even soundproofing would be tested with a scream. I forced myself to calm down, to take two deep breaths before continuing.

"Care to tell me what you and the others are up to with Wraith?" I asked in almost a normal tone.

Another frown creased his features, this time with traces of confusion. "What do you mean?"

More deep breaths. I hadn't breathed this much in months. "You all seem . . . inordinately attentive to him. Like you don't notice anyone else."

That also wasn't subtle, but it was the best I could muster, since every fiber of me wanted to grab Bones and see if shaking him would snap him out of this.

His frown cleared and when he spoke, his tone held teasing, affectionate notes. "You're not jealous about me paying attention to him, are you?"

Wow, was karma quick to pay me back for how I'd dismissed Ian's concerns this morning!

"I'm not jealous," I gritted out, switching tactics. "But I thought we agreed that Wraith needed some investigating before we went any further with him."

"Oh, that." Bones waved a hand. "Not necessary. It's obvious he's a good bloke and I'm proud to call him my brother."

My stomach felt like it sank to my knees. His words and my tie into his emotions revealed that this wasn't an act. Bones believed everything he'd said even though the man I loved would never be so blindly trusting. Somehow, Wraith had managed to do the impossible—brainwash a vampire. And not just one; several, judging from Spade, Annette, Mencheres, and Kira's identical behavior. If I didn't need to discover how, so I could reverse it, I'd go downstairs and kill him for screwing with everyone's minds.

Then again, if Wraith was powerful enough to mesmerize other vampires, who knew what tricks he had up his sleeve? I might end up as nothing more than a stain on the floor if I went after him before I knew more about the source of his abilities.

I stared into Bones's eyes and made him a silent promise. *I'll fix this and get the real you back. I don't know how yet, but I will.*

And then I'd kill Wraith, brother-in-law or not. Of course, if he had enough power to brainwash vampires, fabricating his connection to Bones would've been easy. He might have done it as an excuse to get close to everyone. For what purpose, I didn't know, but whatever his motivation, I couldn't let him succeed.

But before I did anything else, I had to cover my tracks. "You're right, I *was* a little jealous of all the attention Wraith was getting," I said, hoping my voice wasn't too husky from the anger roiling in me. "Let me make it up to you. We'll change our plans for Christmas. Instead of just the eight of us, we'll have a big party to officially welcome Wraith into the family."

He smiled with such clear pleasure that my heart twisted. The gorgeous vampire in front of me looked exactly like the man I loved, but somehow, Wraith had buried the real Bones underneath layers I couldn't penetrate.

"That's a smashing idea. He deserves a proper welcome."

Oh, I'd welcome Wraith good and proper, all right. With a lot of lit dynamite, if I got my Christmas wish. But I smiled back, glad beyond measure that the tie between us didn't flow both ways and Bones couldn't sense my emotions.

"Don't you worry, I'll take care of everything."

I banged on the door of room 116. A conversation with the hotel's registration attendant combined with a couple flashes from my gaze had gotten me Ian's room number. Even though I didn't know what alias he'd checked in under, the descriptors of "tall, red-haired, hot, and English" had been enough.

"Open up, Ian!" I called out when another round of banging didn't produce any results.

The door in front of me didn't open, but one at the end of the hall did. A familiar head poked out.

"That's enough, Reaper. You've already woken the dead. No need to rouse everyone else."

Guess I hadn't been given the right room number after all. I started down the hall, but Ian waved me back.

"Let me get my trousers and I'll be right with you."

He disappeared into the room and was back in a minute, sans shirt but wearing the aforementioned pants. To my surprise, he pulled out a key and opened the door I'd been banging on.

"Come in."

I put two and two together, and shook my head in disgust.

"Unbelievable. Something really scary is going on with Bones and the others, but you *still* take the time to get laid."

"Do I smell like I've been shagging?" he said grumpily. "I slept in another room for safety. I told you where I was without knowing if your mind had been bollocksed up, too. So if you'd have shown up with Crispin and broken down this door, I'd have taken that as a sign to run for my life. Since you're alone and appear to be your normal harping self, I take it you're *not* under Wraith's influence."

I was so glad to drop the all-is-well act I'd kept up since last night that I didn't even mind the harping comment. "No, I'm not. But you, I, Denise, and Fabian seem to be the only ones who aren't. It's got to be some sort of spell, but I don't understand how Wraith got one to work on everyone except the four of us."

Ian sighed. "Since I saw you yesterday, I've done nothing but ponder that very question. If I'm right about what we're dealing with, the only thing protecting me is this."

He unzipped his pants and tugged them down. I whirled just in time, barking, "I don't care what you think, your junk does *not* have special abilities. And I already heard about the piercing," over my shoulder.

"That's not what I wanted to show you," he replied in an implacable voice. "Now stop being such a twit and look."

"This better not be one of your sick jokes," I muttered, turning around. Thankfully, the first thing I saw wasn't Ian waggling Mr. One Eye at me, though he didn't seem concerned that his hand didn't totally conceal the flesh behind it. With his free hand, he pointed at a tattoo that was so close to the base of his groin, it melded into his hairline. *So you're a real redhead, too,* ran through my mind before I could help myself.

"Aside from knowing that you appear to have a fetish for decorating your goods, I don't see—"

"This is no ordinary tattoo," he cut me off. "It's a warding symbol. Don't you recognize it from Denise's former markings?"

My gaze narrowed and I did something I would've sworn was impossible not five minutes before—I came closer and knelt down so Ian's groin was in better view. Sure enough, I recognized the symbols. They were smaller, contained in a single circle versus the various markings that had covered Denise's forearms, but unmistakable.

"Wow," I whispered.

He grunted. "If I had a pound for every time a girl said that while in your position."

I sat back and asked the most obvious questions. "Why do you have a tattoo that wards away demonic influence on your *groin*, Ian? And what does this have to do with Bones and the others?"

He gave me an unblinking stare. "Because decades ago, I ran afoul of a demon and didn't want him finding me. Also didn't want that fact bandied about, so I hid my warding spell in a place where most people who saw it wouldn't know its meaning."

My gaze bored into his with equal intensity. "How did you run afoul of a demon? Did you make a deal and then renege?"

"No." For some reason, I believed him, so the single word relieved me. Getting out of a demonic deal was nigh-impossible, and they usually accepted only one form of currency: your soul. Much as Ian rubbed me the wrong way, I wouldn't wish that to be hanging over his head.

"Then what?"

"It's not pertinent," he said crisply. "Suffice it to say that during this time, I discovered demons have their own form of black magic, only theirs makes everyone else's look like child's play."

I swallowed hard. Fabian had spied Wraith sprinkling blood around our property and found the strange symbol in the bedroom. With everyone's bizarre actions the next day, I'd assumed Wraith must be into magic. Looked like I was right, only he'd gone much darker—and more dangerous—than that.

"Wraith's a vampire, not a demon. So how could he wield hell's version of a spell? I've never heard of a vampire doing that, and mastering a demonic enchantment strong enough to enthrall other vampires should be way beyond his pay grade, from the feel of his aura."

Ian smiled, cold and tight. "Denise feels like an ordinary human, yet she's much more than that, isn't she?"

It hit me what Ian was driving at. He thought Wraith got his additional power through the same method that had made Denise far more than human. If he was right, it explained why Wraith only felt like an average vampire though he could wield a spell that even Mencheres wouldn't dare to attempt. I still didn't know why I was unaffected, but it also made sense why Ian, Denise, and Fabian weren't influenced by the demonic magic. Of course, it also meant that Wraith was nearly unstoppable.

"We're so fucked," I breathed.

Ian let out a dry laugh. "That's the first sensible thing you've said all morning."

Eight

I heard Wraith's voice before I got out of the car. Its melodic cadence combined with my favorite accent should've sounded soothing. Instead, it was like nails on a chalkboard. *Don't you ever tire of listening to yourself talk?* I wondered irritably, but affixed a bright smile on my face when I came through the door.

That smile almost cracked when I saw Wraith seated on an ottoman as though it were a throne. He'd moved it so that he was near the large fireplace, the glow from it playing over his features and making him look even more ethereal. Wraith wore another flowery shirt under his jacket, lace spilling out over the cuffs to wreath his hands. I'd first thought he picked those shirts to be pretentious, but now I had another idea about why he wore them, and it had nothing to do with an outdated fashion sense.

Wraith smiled at me. "Cat. I trust your trip was fruitful?"

I pulled up a seat next to Bones, who, like everyone else, sat in a semicircle around Wraith, akin to adoring courtiers paying their king homage. It was all I could do not to grab a poker and beat Wraith's head in before I roasted his chestnuts for some real holiday cheer.

"Oh, yeah, I found a few places that I think would work for the party," I said, sticking to the excuse I'd given for running out this morning. "In fact, I want to take Denise and get her opinion on my favorites."

"I'm sure that will be lovely." Wraith stretched out his legs. "Right, then. We were just talking about—"

"I meant now," I cut him off as pleasantly as I could.

His smoky-blue eyes narrowed. "Rather rushed about it, aren't you?"

"It's almost Thanksgiving, so the best places are booking up fast for the winter holidays," I improvised, trying to sound as sincere and obsequious as possible. "I'd be so embarrassed if we had to settle for a substandard facility to hold your introduction party. After all, this is so much more important than a regular Christmas celebration."

It wasn't lost on me that Bones was silent, letting Wraith determine what I would and wouldn't do with my own time. If I'd had any lingering doubts about him being bespelled, that got rid of them. The man I married would tell Wraith to keep his bloody opinions to himself should I ever have an unexpected case of muteness when someone questioned me on my comings and goings. Not sit back quietly and let a stranger muse over whether I was allowed to go out for an afternoon. No one else uttered a peep, either. It was as though they'd been replaced with incredibly lifelike mannequins.

"Do hurry back," Wraith said at last, with an acquiescing flick of his fingers.

If I held this fake smile any longer, my face would crack. "You'll barely notice we were gone."

Denise rose, shooting me a grateful look once her back was turned to Wraith. Spade didn't glance her way or bother saying good-bye. Neither did Bones, another piece of evidence that nothing but an otherworldly spell could account for this type of behavior from a vampire to his wife. I stared at Bones as long as I dared, wishing I could find an excuse to get him to leave, too. But Wraith wouldn't allow that, and telling him where to shove it would clue him in that I wasn't under his dirty little enchantment. Plus, in Bones's current state, he probably would refuse to leave if Wraith didn't want him to.

Rage flared through me, which I stuffed back with promises of another time, another place. "See you all soon," I got out, and followed Denise out the door.

Fabian already floated by the car, to my relief. He would come with us while his ghostly girlfriend, Elisabeth, stayed here to keep an eye on things. "Get in," I whispered at him.

Fabian disappeared and then reappeared in the back-seat in the time it took me to blink. I pulled out of the driveway nice and slow, no telltale squealing of tires or flying gravel to betray my sense of urgency. Denise was also so tense that I couldn't hear a word of her thoughts. A good thing, too, since if I couldn't, then Mencheres and Bones couldn't, either, and they wouldn't relay anything to Wraith. Only when we were miles away did my white-knuckle grip on the steering wheel lessen.

"Ian's got a theory about what's going on," I said, breaking the silence.

"Well?" she prodded.

I got onto the freeway, heading toward Asheville. "You're not going to like it, because it means that nei-ther of us can go back."

"What? No!" she said at once. "I'm not leaving Spade with some dick that's got him acting like a robot for God knows what reason—"

"You think I like leaving Bones?" I cut her off. "I know exactly how hard this is, but if we ever want to see our husbands without them being the equivalent of Wraith's wind-up toys, we need to work together."

Her mouth remained mulishly set, but she asked, "What's Ian's theory?" without further argument.

I sighed and reached out, pulling up the sleeve of Denise's cardigan to expose the dark, star-shaped marking on her forearm.

"Wraith's spell is rooted in demonic magic, and the reason he can wield it is because under his long lacy sleeves, we think he has a pair of demon brands, too."

Denise paled until our skin tones almost matched. I returned my attention to the road, not wanting to add to my woes with a high-speed collision.

Fabian recovered first. "If Wraith was also branded by a demon, then like Denise, he now has all the powers of that demon. He'll be almost impossible to kill!"

"Bull's-eye," I noted dryly.

"We have a knife made of demon bone. Stab it through his eyes and he'll die, same as I would," Denise said, still sounding dazed by the information.

I gave her a jaded glance. "Where's that knife now, huh?"

"Spade has it locked up for safety reasons," she murmured, then added, "I don't know where, and I can't ask with him being all spell-addled. Fuck!"

I nodded. "That's just what I've been saying."

Fabian cleared his throat, which, for someone lacking a physical esophagus, was his way of politely telling us to pay attention.

"That could be, ah, rectified."

I met his gaze in the rearview mirror. "I'm glad you think so, because part of our plan involves you helping us search Spade's many houses to find it."

A delicate cough. "That's not necessary. The same, ahem, *material* is right here."

"Fabian, get to the point, please? Your beating around the bush isn't making any sense," I said, exasperated.

"Yes it is," Denise replied, drawing out each word. "He means we have all the demon bone we need in my body."

Nine

Ian's brows shot up. I repeated my statement more slowly, regretting this course of action but agreeing that it was necessary.

"We need to cut something off Denise and use her bones to make a weapon against Wraith."

"Oh, I heard you the first time." Ian's mouth twisted as he looked at Denise. "I was just pondering how much your husband will beat my arse when he's back to himself and hears about this."

"Believe me, I won't tell him if you won't," she replied with a touch of grim humor. Then her tone hardened. "But this changes things. We'll carve two knives, and you'll take one while I'll take the other, because I'm going back to Spade."

"You can't. If Wraith finds out you're like him, he'll kill you on the spot!" I snapped.

"Better if we find a way to lure the others away from him first and then attack him," Ian said, backing me up.

Denise let out a snort. "You guys are forgetting what happened when I killed the demon who branded me. It made everything he'd done to me permanent. If we kill Wraith without undoing his spell first, we risk everyone staying exactly as they are *for the rest of their lives.*"

The truth of that rolled over me like an avalanche. I'd thought it would be hard getting Wraith away from the equivalent of five bespelled vampire bodyguards so we could stab his eyes out, but what we'd need to do instead made that seem easy.

I let out a groan. "We have to find the demon that branded him, and hope to God he wants his power back."

Ian snorted. "Poor analogy, Reaper."

Whatever. I'd hope to hell if that would improve our odds, but the fact remained that only the demon could remove the effects of the brands. Without those, Wraith would be a regular vampire. And if he'd been hiding from that demon, he'd soon be a dead vampire. Even if the demon did the unimaginable and let him live, I wouldn't.

"I can't chase after the demon; I killed one," Denise continued. "I'm betting their kind is pretty intolerant of that. But you two can, and in the meantime, I'll keep an eye on Wraith. If he tries to hurt anyone, I'll have that knife, but I'll only use it as a last resort."

I hated this plan. It left everyone I loved at the mercy of a man who'd used a demonic spell to steal their free will for reasons unknown, but they couldn't be altruistic reasons. It would be a race to see who was successful first: Wraith in implementing his end game, or me and Ian in finding the demon who branded him with the power to cast such a spell, among other abilities. I shuddered, but Denise was right. If Bones—the *real* Bones!—were here now, he'd tell me he would rather be dead than mentally enslaved for the rest of his life. Knowing the others as I did, they'd say the same, too.

Winner really would take all in this race.

"Then it's settled," Ian said. "On to the next task at hand."

His gaze slid over Denise with cool calculation, and though she stayed ramrod-straight, I flinched. I knew he was deciding which part of her to slice off.

"Your lower leg will do," he said, as casual as discussing which cut of steak he'd prefer for dinner. "The bone's long enough that we should be able to fashion two blades, and thick enough that it shouldn't splinter while we're carving them. Femur would be better, but then you'd bleed like a cut snake."

"Your concern for the carpet is touching," Denise muttered.

He flashed her a genial smile. "I'm not fretting over the carpet. We're doing this in the tub, but the more blood you lose, the longer it'll take you to grow that back."

He had a point. Lop off anything on a vampire except their head, and it would grow back in two minutes flat. Denise's regenerative abilities were less rapid, but in their own way, more impressive. She looked human, but now she was in every way the same as the demon who'd branded her, right down to her bones. Denise actually *could* survive being beheaded. Cockroaches had nothing on her.

She let out a long sigh. "Let's get this over with."

Denise started toward the bathroom, but Ian's voice stopped her. "I'm not cutting into you until you're under my sway, so you won't feel it. Think I'm a sadist?"

"Yes," she said, the word "duh" implied in her tone.

He laughed. "You have me there, poppet, but I have certain standards when it comes to women. I don't hurt them unless they enjoy it, and you won't enjoy this."

Denise crossed her arms. "Look, Ian, I appreciate the semi-concern, and no offense intended, but I doubt you have enough juice to put me under—"

She stopped talking when his gaze changed from turquoise to sizzling emerald. Power flashed over me, fast as a snapping whip and strong enough to sting like one. I blinked. Either Ian had been doing some supernatural workouts lately, or he'd held back on showing me the true scope of his power before. By the time he'd crossed the room to Denise, her eyes were wide and staring into nothing, all without Ian even needing to speak.

"We'll see how much you question my juices when you wake up with a freshly regenerated leg," he muttered, picking her up and slinging her over his shoulder. "Come along. I'm not doing this alone. Besides, Denise isn't the only one getting some work done now. You are, too."

"Me?" I asked as I followed him into the bathroom.

Ian set Denise in the tub and then looked up at me, smiling wolfishly as he pulled out a silver knife.

"Your not-quite-dead, vampire-who-eats-vampires status may have kept Wraith's spell from working on you thus far, but we're taking no chances. I'm carving a warding tattoo on you, and setting it with silver-infused ink, so brace yourself. This will hurt."

Ten

Thanksgiving Day. I should've been home, gathered around a table filled with food that most of us would eat only because it was tradition. Instead, I was with Ian at a strip club whose broken neon sign advertised full nudity. Guess G-strings were considered too modest for this establishment. I only wished the managers were as strict in their policy about cleanliness. I'd been in some sleazy places before, but this one made me glad I couldn't catch any of the germs that were no doubt crawling over every inch of the interior. I didn't even drink my gin and tonic, because the glass still had clear impressions of other people's lips on it.

The dancer's thoughts revealed she was no happier to be here than I was, but she dutifully went about her act, gyrating, bending over, and otherwise showing enough of her assets to prove that the outdoor sign wasn't false advertising. I waited until she was finished and then waved her over, stuffing some twenties into her garter—the only piece of clothing she wore. She relayed her thanks with a wide-stance hip thrust that I looked away from. I didn't do it to see more of her lady parts; I did it since she'd been wondering how she was going to afford taking her son to the doctor because his cold hadn't gotten any better.

Ian snickered. "For that much money, you could've had a few lap dances."

"Stuff it," I said wearily.

Where do you go if you're looking for demons? Every place humans were most likely to be feeling desperate, according to Ian. Because of the unthinkable terms of a demonic deal, the people who were willing to agree to them felt like they had either nowhere else to turn, or nothing to lose. Over the past week, we'd spent enough time in hospices, homeless shelters, county jails, and mental-health facilities to make me thoroughly depressed for more reasons than not finding a hint of that telltale sulfur scent. Tomorrow, if we still struck out, we'd leave the state to hit other potential demonic hotspots, like casinos and the stock exchange.

On a holiday like Thanksgiving, strip clubs were filled with the very picture of dejection, with a generous side order of the required desperation. I could even smell it on them beneath the alcohol fumes and other less than aromatic scents from the club. Not that I pointed fingers. I knew from experience that being lonely on a holiday felt more intense than other days of the year.

Case in point: my current mood. Either depression was catching, or it was getting harder to stop brooding about the last conversation I'd had with Bones. I'd covered up the real reason behind my absence with an excuse about my old job needing my assistance. Normally, when you quit a job, your former employer couldn't call you back, but my occupation had been hunting the undead for a covert brand of Homeland Security. It was feasible that I could've been reactivated for a mission. Plus, let's face it: I had a track record, so my abrupt departure wouldn't be that unheard of. Wraith might be suspicious, but he could only guess that I was really after him instead of helping my old team catch some rogue undeads.

But oh, Bones's voice when I called to say I wasn't coming back for a while. I didn't know if his coldness had been influenced by the spell or by a very real sense of betrayal. I'd sworn never to take off again like this, but how could I explain that I had to break that promise because he wasn't really *Bones* at the moment?

I couldn't, so, feeling heartsick, I'd hung up as quickly as possible.

When the door opened, momentarily letting a blaze of sunshine into the darkened establishment, I almost didn't bother looking up. Seeing another face mirroring my own emotional mix of determination and despondency would only hammer home how much I wished circumstances were different. But I did look, and though there was nothing unusual about the young man's appearance, a wave of acrid air blew in with him.

Air that stank like sulfur.

My spirits lifted in a blink. Who'd have thought running into a demon would make someone's day, but I almost clapped in delight. I didn't wait for Ian, but bolted toward the newcomer, smiling broadly.

Maybe it was my smile that kept him from sensing danger. Maybe he hadn't yet noticed that I didn't have a heartbeat, or he felt secure because, compared to demons, vampires were easy to kill. Either way, he didn't fight when I grabbed him and hustled him back outside.

"We need to talk," I told him.

The demon laughed, staring me up and down. "I normally don't like room-temperature meat, but for you, I'll—"

His dubiously flattering statement was cut short when Ian appeared, wrenching the demon's arms behind his back.

"As the lady told you," Ian said pleasantly, "we need to have a word with you."

The demon's light brown eyes began to fill with red. "You don't know who you're fucking with, vampires."

I reached into my jacket and pulled out a long, thin knife, holding it near the demon's eye.

"As a matter of fact, we know exactly who we're fucking with."

Eleven

We flew him onto the roof of a taller building for more privacy. There, Ian and I forced the demon to sit and then tied him to a metal air-conditioning vent. Being in direct sunlight would weaken the demon. Plus, the ropes were entwined with rock salt, so if our new friend had the ability to dematerialize, this would mute it. It would also discourage struggling. The ropes were over his clothes now, but squirming would bring them in direct contact with the demon's exposed neck, and he wouldn't like the results.

"We have questions," Ian said once we'd finished. "Answer them without lying, and you'll walk away safe and sound."

The demon glanced at the knife again and whistled. "Bone of the brethren. Aren't *you* the naughty pair for having that? Still, the knife is only good for killing and

I can't answer questions if I'm dead. You'd get me to talk faster by offering me cash."

He wanted us to bribe him? "I saw a church a few blocks up. Maybe I'll grab some holy water and *then* we'll chat," I snapped.

The demon laughed. "That stuff does nothing to my kind. You watch too many movies."

Not the first time I'd been accused of that, but it would be really helpful if the movies got things right for once. Of course, that didn't mean I was out of scare-tactic options.

I pulled out two salt shakers I'd packed into my jacket where my silver knives used to go. Different creatures required different weapons, after all.

"Now how about we get serious? Vampire by the name of Wraith made a deal with one of your kind. I want to know who."

The demon scoffed. "How should I know? It wasn't me, that's all I can say."

I threw a handful of salt onto his face. It bubbled his skin up like it was acid, but I knelt and clapped my hand over his mouth to silence his scream. "Don't toy with me, I am so not in the mood," I hissed in his ear.

Muffled grunts sounded against my hand. Cautiously, I lifted it, but he didn't scream again. He spit out some salt before glaring at me.

"We're demons, not Amway. It's not like I can pick up a phone and find out who's got a deal out on your vamp."

"You're supposed to have the power to grant just about any request, yet you expect me to believe you can't find a name?"

I wagged the salt shakers threateningly as I spoke. The demon sighed. "Keep seasoning me all you want, but I still can't tell you who has the deal on that vamp. It's not like we update a worldwide Excel sheet every time we contract a soul."

"But you're demons!" I burst out. "Scary, powerful, soul-snatching scourges of the underworld! How can you *not* do something as simple as keep in touch about who you brand?"

A shrug. "We're independent contractors. Don't like it? Complain to management. Maybe dialing 666 will get you someone."

I wanted to fling the rest of the salt on him out of sheer frustration, but his words held the ring of truth. I guess it had been too much to hope that snagging one demon would mean we'd find out who'd branded Wraith. Over a week later, and we still had nothing to show for our efforts. Despair coursed through me until I felt like I was choking on it. The demon's head lolled back and he inhaled.

"Mmm, smells delicious. If you're determined to find the demon's name, there's a way to bypass all that pesky hunting."

I wrestled back my gloom enough to let out a bark of laughter. "Let me guess: it involves dealing away my soul?"

He lifted his head. "Again, I don't make the rules. I just play by them, and the rules say I can't tap into wish-granting without the right form of deposit."

Yeah, I felt desperate and tired and scared shitless about what might be happening to Bones, but that wasn't the answer. I'd find another way.

"No deal," I said coldly. "And since you're not able to tell us anything useful . . ."

I put down the salt to grab the bone knife again, but Ian shook his head. "We agreed to let him go if he told us the truth, and I believe he did."

"If we let him go, he's going to keep *damning* people," I pointed out, in case he'd somehow forgotten that.

Ian waved his hand. "Both of us act according to our natures. I drink blood. He collects souls. Just because we have different methodologies doesn't mean I'm going to dishonor our agreement."

Only Ian could so casually describe what a demon did as a methodology. The demon wagged his finger at me. "You were going to kill me despite your promise. Liar, liar, pants on fire! Heh, takes me back to my days in the pit. Everyone's pants were on fire there."

He laughed at his own joke. Unbelievably, Ian joined in. I stared at the two, wishing I could stab at least one of them and not being sure who I wanted it to be at the moment.

"Since there's nothing more to talk about, I'm leaving," I said with as much dignity as I could muster. They could keep chortling away if they wanted, but I had better things to do. Like figure out how we were going to find one demon amidst thousands.

Ian cut the bonds from the demon and he stood, cracking his back as though relieving a kink. Then, to my amazement, Ian pulled out a large wad of cash from his coat and peeled off several bills.

"This is for your silence about what we discussed," he said, holding out the money. The demon pocketed it in a blink.

Not only were we letting the demon go free, we were paying him for telling us absolutely nothing. I gave a last disgusted shake of my head and turned around, heading for the exit.

I was about to yank open the door to the roof when the demon said, "You know, there is one other way you might be able to narrow down your search."

I froze before slowly turning around. Ian's brow arched, but the demon said nothing else. Instead, he stared at the lump of folded bills Ian was about to put back in his coat.

Ian snorted and peeled off another few. "This is all you get on good faith. Impress me, and you'll get more."

The demon pocketed the money before glancing around, as if fearing other demons would ascend from the floor of the roof. Then he lowered his voice.

"I'm not supposed to consort with vampires, but I like your style—and your money—so bring me one of the spelled vamps, and I'll tell you the power required to conjure that sort of enchantment. You'll know then if the demon who branded your boy is medium-level, a higher up, or one of the original Fallen."

Ian pulled off a thick stack of bills. The demon's eyes bugged, but before he could snatch it, Ian held it out of reach.

"If you're truly able to determine the power level of Wraith's brander, and help us find him or her, I'll give you triple this. My word on it."

The demon pulled out a piece of paper and pen, then scribbled on it. I came close enough to see that it was a series of symbols followed by the word "Bal-chezek."

"My true name," he said, holding it out to Ian. "Draw this in unsoiled blood, say my name three times, and I'll appear."

"Don't you just have a cell phone number you can give us?" Demons and their love of bloody rituals.

He slid a jaded glance my way. "I'm guessing when you call, you'll be pressed for time, so I'm giving you the no-waiting-required method. Besides, you never need to worry about coverage bars or dropped calls with this."

Good point, but I had one more question. "By unsoiled blood, do you mean freshly shed instead of bagged plasma?"

Balchezek exchanged a glance with Ian, who rolled his eyes. "Times like this I feel old," Ian muttered, to a grunt of agreement from the demon. "He means virgin's blood."

I bristled. "Are you trying to say that if a chick gives it up, she's considered *soiled*? What kind of sexist bullshit is—"

"It can be male blood, too," Balchezek said, winking at me. "Whatever turns you on."

Twelve

Ian and I had just made it back to our hotel room when Fabian appeared without so much as a chill in the air to warn of his presence.

"Where have you been? I've been waiting for hours!"

"Sorry I'm late for curfew, Mom," I mocked, then stilled at his expression. "What happened?"

The ghost looked so stricken I thought my knees might buckle. Was it Bones? Oh God, if something happened to him. . .

"Cat, you have been disowned," Fabian said.

I waited a beat, but he didn't follow that up with anything else. Amidst my overwhelming relief that no one was dead, I was confused. Especially when Ian muttered, "Bugger," the same way someone else would say "fuck."

"Um, I haven't talked to my mother in two weeks, but we left things on good terms, and though my uncle and I aren't speaking at the moment, I don't think—"

"He means Crispin cut you off from his line," Ian interrupted, shooting me a look filled with grimness and pity.

That jelly-kneed feeling returned with a vengeance. I sat down, trying to absorb the information without doing anything ridiculous, like crying.

It wasn't fear that made my emotions reel with this news, though Bones cutting me off from his line was considered a worse punishment than execution, in the vampire world. It left me on the lowest level of undead society, fair game for anyone who wanted to mete out cruelty without chance of repercussions. No, that's not what upset me the most. It was the knowledge that this was the closest Bones could come to divorcing me. Under vampire law, we would be married until one of us was all the way dead, but this was his public statement that I meant less than nothing to him. Hell, Mencheres hadn't even cut off his former wife, Patra, before she died, and she'd been trying to kill him.

"You know this isn't Crispin," Ian said. He sat next to me and patted my leg in a kindly fashion. "Wraith should hope we find the demon who branded him. He'd die easier under that bloke's hand than under Crispin's when he's back to himself and hears of this."

"I know." My voice was thick, because I did know that, but the knowledge that Wraith's spell could force Bones to do this meant it truly had taken over every part of him. What if we couldn't reverse the spell to get him back? That question was more terrifying than any danger this proclamation put me in.

Fabian fluttered over, doing his own version of a sympathetic pat by brushing his hands through my shoulders.

"I'm afraid there's more. After he declared you to be cut off, he designated Wraith to assume Mastership of his line should anything befall him."

I bolted up so fast that my upper body was briefly sheathed inside the ghost. "Sonofabitch! We've been wondering why Wraith would go through all this trouble to bewitch everyone, but the fucker must be doing it for power! If Bones dies, then Wraith slides into his place, ruling not only Bones's line, but co-ruling one of the largest and strongest lines in the vampire nation with Mencheres."

Oh, the slippery bastard! Wraith could never get in a position of such power through force. Bones would crush him in a fight, not to mention if he didn't, Mencheres would. But put the demonic whammy on both men's minds, plus on the closest members of their inner circle, and Wraith would be sitting pretty just as soon as Bones had a lethal accident.

Which, I had no doubt, Wraith intended to happen soon.

"This changes who we need to bring to Balchezek," I said, pacing. "It's gotta be Bones."

We'd originally decided to snatch Annette. With her lower power level and lack of a spouse to watch over her, she would've been easier to rescue—or kidnap, as she wouldn't want to go. But though Bones was stronger than me or Ian, I couldn't sit back and hope Wraith would wait for us to outmaneuver him before he killed Bones to put the last piece of his plan into place.

Ian sighed. "And here I was really looking forward to it being Annette."

"Don't chicken out now," I warned him.

He shot me a measured look as he stood. "I told you once before: Crispin is one of the few people I'd fight to keep from harm, even at the cost of my own life. Tomorrow, I'll prove it."

I stared at him, noting the hard line of his jaw and the uncompromising gleam in his vibrant turquoise gaze.

"You do that, and I take back every nasty thing I've ever said about you."

He grinned, his mood changing from serious to wicked in an instant. "Why? I'm all those things and more."

I shook my head. Ian was more proud of his depravity than anyone I'd met, but if he helped me pull Bones out from under four bespelled vampires and one demonically-enhanced vamp, I'd shower him with prostitutes and porn while swearing he was an angel.

However, Mencheres could decapitate us with his mind, and on my best day I couldn't take Bones in a fight, so neither of us might live through tomorrow. We were going up against our friends and loved ones, which made us operate under the constraint of not killing anyone. It didn't take a crystal ball to know that with Wraith's spell pulling their strings, we wouldn't be shown the same consideration.

Oh well. Time to ante up on that " 'til death do us part" section of my vows. Living forever sounded boring anyway.

I strode up the gravel road that led to my house. Bare tree limbs swayed in the breeze and the air was crisp enough to see my breath, if I had any. Today was aptly referred to as Black Friday, when malls and Walmarts became bargain war zones for holiday shoppers hunting for the best deals. My war zone consisted of a steep wooded hill with two picturesque cabins at the top of it; my coveted prize the brown-haired vampire who'd publicly disowned me.

I knew when my presence was detected by the sudden hush of conversation in the main house above. Fine. Wraith's voice had been grating on my nerves anyhow.

"Honey, I'm home!" I called out loudly, quickening my pace.

By the time I reached the top of the hill, the front door was open and Wraith stood framed in it. My face stretched into a smile that felt more like a sneer. No need to pretend I was under his demonic thrall anymore.

"Well, hi there, bro. Couldja send the hubby on out?"

"You are not welcome here, Cat," he said, as if *he* owned the place.

"*Au contraire*, my good man. Cut off or not, I'm still Bones's legal wife, and vampire law states that wherever one spouse is, the other automatically has an invitation, too. So either send Bones out, or I'm coming in."

The bottom of my black jacket rustled in the cold wind, but not the top. That was too weighted down with weapons. Wraith had either heard enough about my reputation to guess that, or he could tell from my expression that "no" wasn't an acceptable answer to me. He disappeared inside the house, and seconds later, another vampire came out, but not the one I was here for.

Mencheres stood in the doorway, his Egyptian features schooled into hard, unreadable planes. It only took one look into his eyes to know that Wraith had ordered him to kill me.

Thirteen

The sudden overwhelming pressure on my neck came before I could even attempt to run, not that running would have done any good. Mencheres didn't need me to stand still to rip my head off.

But just as quickly as that awful squeezing started, it stopped. A red dot appeared on Mencheres's forehead, darker gore spattering the doorway behind him. He dropped to his knees, the strangest look on his face as he slowly pitched forward.

"Nice shot, Ian," I muttered, and then ran toward the door. The single silver bullet wouldn't kill Mencheres, but silver took much longer to heal, buying us precious time until his brains unscrambled and he regained consciousness.

And once that happened, if we were still here, we'd be toast.

Someone crashed into me right as I cleared the threshold. It happened so fast I didn't see who it was, but the softer flesh made my attacker either Annette or Kira. Her momentum propelled us into the nearest wall and pain thudded through me from blows I made no move to defend against. Blond hair caught my eye as my attacker bent to rip her fangs through my shoulder, missing my neck because I twisted away at the last second.

Kira, then. She wasn't armed, though, so while this hurt, it wouldn't kill me. I let her tear into my skin and pummel me while I reached around to grab the Glock from the back of my jeans. Then I whipped the gun up and shot her through the head.

Her instant flaccidity was replaced with a larger, harder form barreling into us next. Kira's bloody head pressed against my face, blinding me from seeing my latest assailant. But brutal punches that snapped my ribs and reverberated through my body in fiery waves told me who this was. Only one person hit that hard.

Bones.

"Now!" I screamed, wedging Kira's limp form out from between us.

Glass shattered in rapid succession as Ian shot the percussion grenades through the downstairs windows. The subsequent explosions felt like bombs going off in my brain, but I'd packed enough wax into my ears to take the edge off the worst of the effects. The other vampires, with their supersensitive hearing, weren't as lucky. Bones stopped pureeing my insides to clutch his head, blood leaking out from his ears. Behind his bent form, I saw Spade, Annette, and Wraith doing the same thing. Denise wasn't down here. Fabian had snuck into her room last night to warn her to stay away from the main floor once the action started.

I used that second of distraction to plug a bullet into Wraith's head next, watching with extreme satisfaction as crimson exploded onto his long, blond locks. If only I could finish the job with the bone knife, but I needed the spell reversed, so Wraith had to stay alive.

Bones lifted his head. Blood still stained his ears, but he'd recovered from the debilitating effect of the percussion grenades. Green sizzled from his gaze, and his mouth opened in a snarl as he launched himself at me. Over his shoulder, I saw that Spade and Annette were also shaking off the effects and coming at me with murderous expressions.

I raised the gun, but before I could pull the trigger, the Glock was wrenched from my hand with a snap of power that broke my wrist. Goddamn it, Bones was using his fledgling telekinesis against me! I could only hope he didn't have enough of it to take off my head, or shooting Mencheres would have been a waste of time. That concern cleared out of my mind when Bones vaulted upward the instant before he was about to crash into me. I'd braced for the impact of his tall, muscled frame flattening me against the wall, but instead got a kick to the face that snapped my neck and filled my vision with red.

Agony flared from every facial nerve ending, combined with sickening crunching noises that confirmed my bones had shattered as thoroughly as the glass from the front windows. I resisted the instinctive urge to protect myself from further injury, knowing Bones would move in for the kill. Instead, I flung myself forward, smacking my face against a rock-hard chest. The contact shot more fireworks of pain into my skull, but tucked me under the deadly arm that had been arcing toward my neck.

My vision might be bloody and my face in ruins, but my legs worked *fine*, and Bones had made an unusual mistake by widening his stance when he tried to wrest my head off. I took advantage of that and slammed my knee upward, using all my supernatural strength to make merciless contact with his groin. That brought him to his knees, but before I could pull out my other gun, something hard slammed into my still-healing face.

Amidst another blast of pain and crunching sounds that I never wanted to hear again, I caught a glimpse of

Spade winding up for a second blow. I ducked, his pale hand smashing through the wall behind me instead, but then twin sledgehammers connected with my sides. Bones had recovered from my nutcracker kick and was back on the offensive.

I couldn't block an attack from above *and* below. Not without lethal means, and those weren't an option. I couldn't scramble away, either. The wall blocked me from behind and three pissed off vampires blocked my front. All I could do was hope to God they were too busy attacking me to stop and run for a silver knife. After a few moments of duck, twist, punch, repeat, I realized something strange: Bones and Spade weren't fighting like their usual, deadly selves. Their skills seemed to have diminished to the same level as Annette's. Otherwise, I couldn't have held them off as well as I was doing.

A boom sounded and Spade flew across the room, a large, smoking hole now in his midsection. Bones whirled to assess this new threat, but I hauled him back as Ian jumped through the ruins of the front window. About time.

"Hallo, all!" Ian announced. With a savage grin, he tossed aside the still-smoking bazooka and leapt at Annette.

More backup would've meant less risk, but aside from one trusted vampire who wasn't answering his phone, all my strongest and closest allies were the people I was fighting against. Denise couldn't afford to blow her cover by coming to our defense, so she helped the only way she could—by staying out of the way.

When Ian reached Annette, he threw her across the room with enough force to send her smashing through my china cabinet. Amidst the sounds of yet more glass shattering, I heard his shout.

"What are you waiting for? Get Crispin out of here!"

Did Ian think I'd stopped to do my nails? I was busy trying to fend off another attempt to separate my head from the rest of my body. But I ducked under Bones's latest overhand swipe and grabbed him in a bear hug, wincing as the close contact meant his body punches landed with even more devastating effect. He might not be fighting with his usual skill, but he hit just as hard. Then I mustered my power and blasted us through the empty windows, Ian's roar to Spade filling my ears.

"No you don't! You're staying right here!"

More sounds of violence ensued before the wind and my velocity snatched them away. Annette couldn't fly, so Spade was the only vampire left with the ability to chase us, and it was up to Ian to stop him. Even if Annette and Spade didn't overpower him, Mencheres would wake up any minute. If that happened before Ian got away, he wouldn't live long enough to scream before he'd be missing his head. I didn't care how proud he was of his sins; for this, I *did* take back every derogatory thing I'd ever said about Ian.

Bones fought to break my grip on him, but I didn't let go no matter that my entire torso felt like it had been run over by a truck. I couldn't defend against his barrage of blows and stop him from flying back to Wraith at the same time. It was hard enough to concentrate over the pain to keep propelling us upward. We were miles from the cabin now, but we needed to be even farther away. Too far for Mencheres or anyone else to pick up our trail and follow.

When Bones abruptly stopped his assault, I felt a second of relief that changed at once to alarm. He'd never give up this easily. That was made clear when his hands, no longer curled into punishing fists, slid over me with ruthless, seeking efficiency.

And pulled out one of the silver knives I'd tucked inside my coat.

Our faces were almost level, so I locked eyes with him as that blade came toward my chest. His gaze was still flashing green, his aura cracking with lethal intent, but I couldn't defend myself without letting go of him. If I did, he'd return to Wraith, and I'd be condemning him to death just as surely as if I twisted a knife into his heart.

If these were my last moments on earth, I'd spend them fighting to save him with everything I had. If our roles were reversed, I knew he'd do the same.

The blade broke my skin, sliding into my chest with the sensation of fire made into metal. My body's response to silver grazing my heart was instant. All my power seemed to abandon me, causing my velocity to evaporate. Bones and I began to drop out of the sky, but instead of pushing him away to save myself, I used the last of my strength to tighten my arms around him.

"I love you," I managed to get out amidst the overwhelming pain. As last words went, there weren't any I'd rather say.

Something flickered in his gaze. That blazing emerald glare became flecked with dark brown and his aura fragmented, like an invisible force had struck it with enough force to shatter it. Instead of twisting the knife and ending my life, he pulled it out of my chest—and rammed it into his own.

"No!" I screamed, grabbing for the blade while clutching him with my other arm. Our descent slowed as my power flooded back now that the knife was out of my heart. His failed, the silver sapping his strength like supernatural kryptonite. Only my frantic grip on the hilt kept him from turning the blade and shredding his heart, ensuring true death.

"Kitten." The word was rasped so low I almost didn't hear it above the whoosh of wind. "You have to let me die. Now, while I still have her contained!"

I didn't know what he meant and I didn't care. I pulled the knife free, flinging it aside in revulsion. Bones made a ragged noise and his face twisted, as though he were somehow in more pain without the silver in his heart than with it.

"You're not going to die," I swore, then pressed my mouth to his for a kiss filled with all the love, pain, fear, and frustration of the past several days.

I was still kissing him when I pulled out my other gun and shot him through the head.

Fourteen

The Jiffy Lube station had closed months ago, judging from the layer of dust on the concrete and metal fixtures. But after a few modifications, its underground work area with reinforced walls and thick beams was the perfect place to restrain a vampire. I'd had to shoot Bones in the head again after he healed from the first wound and woke up in another murderous mood, but now he was safely tucked away in what used to be the oil-change undercarriage of the facility, enough weighty chains wound around him to force an average vampire to his knees.

Bones wasn't close to average, though. He stood ramrod-straight and glared at me, his bright green gaze vowing revenge. Whatever flicker of emotion had led him to stop before twisting that knife in me was long gone, much to my regret. But as soon as Ian—who'd survived the fight in one piece, to my relief—was done drawing those bloody symbols on the ground, we'd know what sort of demon we had to chase to reverse the spell Bones was under.

"You were gone less than thirty minutes. How'd you get a couple pints of *that* type of blood so fast?" I wondered. Then my gaze narrowed. "You didn't kill anyone, did you?"

He sat back on his haunches to give me a sardonic look. "I'd never let a perfectly good virgin go to waste that way. Swung by a middle school and collected from a few students. They'll never remember it. Neither will their teacher."

I hated the idea of stealing blood from preadolescents, but we were too pressed for time.

"There," Ian said, drawing the last of the symbols.

"What do you think you're doing?" Bones asked, speaking his first words since he told me to let him die.

Ian didn't reply. He stepped outside the circle and glanced at me.

"Let's hope none of the students I picked were the experimental type." Then he said "Balchezek" three times.

"Stop!" Bones snapped, straining against his chains. The metal creaked but they held. That was why Ian and I had spent most of the night setting up this place.

Nothing stirred in the circle with the bloody symbols, but a brunet man stepped out from behind one of the support beams as casually as if he'd been there all along.

"You called?" Balchezek said.

I let out a sigh of relief. Part of me had wondered if the demon made up the whole summoning ritual and we'd be wasting our time attempting it. Good to know that avarice still meant something to members of the netherworld.

But just in case the demon tried to pull anything, like bringing uninvited friends with him, I had the bone knife within easy reach.

Ian had something else within reach. He drew his thumb along the side of a thick pile of hundred-dollar bills like he was shuffling cards.

"Hallo, Balchezek. If you want these, then look over our mate here and tell us what level of beastie we're going after."

"You shouldn't be here," Bones said, spitting the words in the demon's direction.

"I take it this is the vamp you want me to check out?"

Balchezek walked over to Bones, whistling through his teeth as he got closer. "I can tell you one thing right off. He isn't under a spell like you're thinking. He's possessed."

"Shut up," Bones hissed.

I blinked in disbelief at the statement and the sound of Bones's voice. It was higher, and sounded like he'd lost his English accent all of a sudden.

"I thought it was impossible for vampires to be possessed. That they have too much inherent power for a disembodied demon to break in and set up shop."

"Normally, yes." Balchezek wagged his finger at Bones, who snarled at him. "But like all rules, that one has an exception. It's a pain-in-the-ass exception, which is one of the reasons why demons avoid possessing vampires, so I'm not surprised you didn't think it was possible."

"What are the reasons demons avoid possession with vampires?" Ian asked.

Bones cursed in that unfamiliar, higher voice and swore terrible punishment if Balchezek continued. The demon ignored that and gave Ian a patient look.

"You're a lot harder to break into, for one. Only a medium- or upper-level demon can do that, and only under very specific circumstances. For another, we like keeping the status quo. If demons started possessing a bunch of vampires, it wouldn't take your kind long to amass and fight back. If our numbers get thinned taking you on, then we'd have a harder time fighting our main opponents."

I inhaled to make sure I hadn't missed anything from Bones before. "He doesn't smell like sulfur. Are you sure he's possessed?"

It would explain how I'd felt like I was dealing with a stranger in Bones's skin ever since that first morning after Wraith's appearance, plus his oddly amateur fighting skills and the abrupt reversal in personality when he'd stabbed himself. But I remembered with a spurt of fear the other thing Bones had told me years ago when we'd encountered a possessed human. *The only way to get rid of a demon is to kill the host.*

"Humans don't have the power to conceal the sulfur smell when a demon takes over. A demon-possessed vamp would. Besides," Balchezek made a circular motion from Bones's face down to his chest. "I can see the demon. She's right here."

She? I stared, but all I saw in the area indicated were my husband's furious features and inches of chains writhing with Bones's efforts to break his bonds.

"Of course *you* can't see her," Balchezek went on. "Consider it demon glamour. But just like vampire glamour works on humans but not other vamps, I can see through it."

My head felt like it was spinning. Reversing a demonic spell had seemed hard enough, but this was so much worse. We couldn't catch a break no matter how hard we tried.

"So several demons decided to pitch their tents in my husband and his best friends." A mirthless laugh escaped me. "That's what you're saying?"

"Nope," Balchezek stated. "Just one."

Fifteen

O ne?" Ian repeated with the same incredulity I felt.

" 'My name is Legion, for we are many,' " Balchezek quoted with an arch smile. "In that case, it was several demons inside one person, but the reverse can happen, too. One demon splits him or herself into several parts and simultaneously possesses different people. It's tricky to do, though, because—"

"Be quiet or I will kill you!" Bones roared, his voice now totally feminine and unrecognizable.

"—you can only branch off into members of your anchor's family," Balchezek went on, flipping Bones the bird. "First you have to be lodged into one person good and tight. That's your anchor. Then you perform a ritual on yourself to split off into members of their family and remote-control them, but as a split, it'll make you appear like a blurry facsimile to other demons. And if all that sounds labor-intensive, it's even harder to do with vampires."

"How so?" I asked almost numbly.

"For starters, you can only possess a vampire if you were already in him when he was human, then hung on through the transformation into becoming undead. You need to be crazy strong to do that, but even stronger to attempt simultaneous possessions of other vampires. The upside is that if you pull it off, you're not limited to only possessing your anchor's human family. You could also go up to the third or fourth generation of your anchor's siring bloodline. You'd need to stay within close proximity to your undead flesh puppets, though, and keep their attention focused on you, or a vampire might grab the reins back."

All those stories Wraith kept telling. Was that his way of keeping everyone's attention on him so he could stay demonically implanted? This sounded too unbelievable even for me, and I'd seen—and done—a lot of freaky stuff in my day. Some of that must have showed on my face, because Balchezek sighed.

"You want me to prove it, don't you? All right. Let's get your boy on top again. He's far enough away from the demon's main anchor that it should be easier for him to pop up. Now, what would really, really upset him?"

I wished I could call a time-out to assimilate all the different pieces of information being thrown at me, but I mumbled my reply without pause.

"Bones briefly grabbed control when we were flying. He stabbed me, but instead of twisting the knife, he yanked it out and stuck it in himself."

And said he had to die *while he still had her contained.* Oh God, Balchezek was right. Bones wasn't under a spell; he was possessed, and I didn't know of any way to get the demon out without killing him.

I swiped away a tear that escaped from my eye. Crying wouldn't do a damn bit of good, and there was no time for it, anyway.

"So stab me," I finished, squaring my shoulders. "In the heart."

Ian walked over, but instead of pulling out one of the silver blades I knew he had on him, he yanked me to him.

"I have another idea," he muttered right before his mouth slanted over mine.

I was so stunned that I didn't move for a few seconds. That was long enough for Ian to grab my ass and plaster my hips to his. His mouth opened, tongue seeking entry, but I wrenched my head away.

"Have you lost your *mind*?" I demanded, slapping him.

Ian grinned. "Reminds me of the day we met. As you recall, I didn't mind you getting rough. Turned me on, in fact."

Then he gripped my hair hard enough to pull off several strands, using that as leverage to latch his mouth onto my neck. I closed my fist and prepared to punch him into next week. "If Crispin's in there, this will enrage him into appearing," Ian whispered near my ear.

Few things were ingrained as deeply into vampires as territoriality. It was strong enough toward anyone a vampire considered to be his, but practically rabid if you threw love into the mix. Plus, I might not luck out and live the next time someone plugged my ticker with silver. A few wrong twitches and it was hello, dirt nap.

I didn't really need proof to know that Bones was possessed, but if making out with Ian gave Bones the chance to stomp on top of the demonic bitch inside him, then I'd do it with gusto.

"Oh, yes, that feels so good," I moaned, and instead of punching Ian, pulled him closer.

Breath tickled my neck as he laughed. "I know. I'm truly gifted."

You're truly narcissistic, I thought, but ground against him and raked my hands through his auburn hair, pulling it hard enough to elicit an approving growl. This wasn't the first time I'd had to make out on command; my old day job playing bait to hunt vampires had practically required it. But it felt beyond weird to have *Ian* nipping and licking my skin while I let out some groans and calls for more.

And though I'd never admit it, not all of my moans were faked. Ian had put his promiscuity to effective use because the bastard was good at what he did.

"Ooh, a sex show." It sounded like Balchezek plunked onto the floor for more comfortable viewing. "Nice. And I thought coming here would be boring."

To better access my neck, Ian yanked my collar away from my shoulder, ripping some buttons loose in the process. Not to be outdone, I tore his shirt all the way open, biting some of the skin it revealed before slapping him across the face twice more. Hard.

"I'm glad you like it rough, because I am going to tear your ass *up.*"

Ian turned his face away from Bones, but I caught his lips twitching. His eyes held a definite sparkle as he yanked the remains of my shirt from me, leaving me only in my bra and jeans. A dried blood stain near the center of my chest was the leftover evidence of how close to death I'd come. Ian bent his head there, licking it.

A low growl came from our left. Chains creaked and rattled. I didn't look in the direction, but pressed Ian's head closer.

"That's right, drink my blood," I said, my voice low and throaty. "Now I'm going to taste yours."

Power crackled through the air, growing stronger and yet also feeling ragged, like edges of broken glass trying to piece back together. I didn't turn toward Bones, but fisted Ian's hair and yanked his head to the side, exposing his pale, taut neck.

More rattling of chains, followed by a feminine hiss. I ignored that, too, licking my lips as if in anticipation of Ian's blood. Then I slowly brought my head down. Angled my face so that the vampire chained to the wall would have the best view of me sinking my fangs into his sire's neck, and then sucked in a mouthful of blood.

But when I swallowed that rich liquid, my moan *really* wasn't faked. It reminded me that I hadn't eaten in over a week, and though I might have been too distracted to think about food, my body clearly hadn't forgotten what it craved. My control cracked and I bit into him again, tearing his flesh in my haste to swallow more of that delicious crimson liquid.

"That's right, you nasty little vixen, bite me harder," Ian urged. He raked his nails down my back and pulled my legs around his waist, supporting me with a firm grip on my ass.

Chains crashed together while that feminine hiss turned into a full-throated, masculine roar.

"Get your bloody hands off my wife!"

Sixteen

I jumped off Ian like he'd burned me, even the lure of more blood unable to keep me from responding to the true sound of my husband's voice. Bones's eyes were glowing emerald-green, the rage in them aimed at Ian, and the currents rippling off him made me nervous that the chains wouldn't hold.

Then Bones looked at me, and that seething rage changed to something else. Pain sliced across my subconscious, so sharp and poignant that I ran those last few steps to him.

"Welcome back," I said, touching his face, one of the few places on him that wasn't weighted down with chains.

He closed his eyes and inhaled near my palm, a spasm crossing his features. "You smell like Ian. Tell me you were only pretending, Kitten, or I'll have to kill him."

I smiled through the sudden pink sheen in my gaze. "Me and Ian? Come on, Bones. You know better."

His mouth twisted. "The pair of you looked very convincing."

"That was the point, wasn't it?" Ian asked, sauntering over. "Though I'll admit to mild enjoyment on my part."

Mild enjoyment? My femininity was affronted but the rest of me could care less. I was too busy staring into Bones's eyes and feeling overwhelming relief that I recognized the person staring back at me.

"So you're not having sex." Balchezek made a noise of disappointment. "Now I *am* bored."

Bones glanced at the demon and then back at me. "He's right about everything. I woke up the morning after Wraith appeared and suddenly I was a spectator in my own body."

"It's easier to possess strong people like vampires when they're asleep. Then their guard is down," Balchezek offered. "Otherwise, she'd need to shed buckets of your blood to weaken you enough to force her way inside. A lot messier that way."

Buckets of blood. I flashed back to Annette's hotel room and her odd behavior the night of Bones's birthday party. So she'd been the first one possessed. Wraith *had* been her attacker, but she hadn't accused him, because everything that had come out of Annette's mouth had been directed by the demon piloting her.

The same demon who was piloting Wraith, if Balchezek was right about him being the demon's main "anchor."

"There are a few things I need to say, Kitten," Bones stated, directing my attention back from piecing together the possession chain. "I don't know how long I'll be able to hold the demon down. She's very strong."

"She's still in there?" The realist in me expected that, but I'd hoped his rage had miraculously booted her out.

"Yes," he replied shortly.

"Of course she is." Balchezek shook his head. "You think I was lying to you?"

I didn't point out that he was a demon, so lies went with the territory. He was our best source of information and I didn't want him leaving in a huff.

"You'll need to record me rescinding my disownment of you and your reinstatement as heir to my line," Bones said, fury skipping across his features before he went on. "I'll also expose Mencheres, Kira, Spade, Annette, and Wraith as being possessed. Once I've done that, give me a silver knife. No one will doubt my statements when they see I'm willing to die for them."

"No!" I said at once, horror flooding through me.

Bones closed his eyes briefly. "I'm sorry it's come to this, but I've no illusions about what must be done. Believe me, I would rather be dead a thousand times over than to again watch as my own hands smash into you because some bitch has control of my body instead of me."

I grabbed his hair less roughly than I had Ian's a few minutes before. "But you stopped her when she put that knife in my heart. You stopped her!"

"Outing yourself and Mencheres as possessed will result in civil war within your line," Ian warned. "Not to mention inviting all your enemies to attack when you're weakened. It will cause a bloodbath, Crispin."

"Ian's right, listen to him," I said, too concerned about Bones to be shocked at those words coming out of my mouth.

"I might not be able to stop her next time she attempts to kill you, and I refuse to risk it," he snapped. "Even now she's ripping at my strength to regain control. You swore, Kitten. Years ago when Mencheres challenged you over whether you could kill me if your situations were reversed, you swore that if I murdered those close to you and wouldn't stop, you would do it.

The demon in me will kill everyone in her way, and you cannot allow that. The only way to stop her is to kill me."

No. No. The words resounded through me so loudly that it took a second to realize someone else was speaking.

" . . . might be another way, but it'll cost you," Balchezek finished.

My gaze swung to the walnut-haired demon. "What? What other way?" If he said it would cost me my soul, God help me, but I might do it.

Bones closed his eyes, wincing a little. "She's getting very restless. Just as I was aware of everything when she had control, so she is listening now. Best not to discuss this in front of me, Kitten."

"That's what I've been saying," Balchezek muttered. He strode out of the room, tossing a "You coming or what?" over his shoulder.

I looked at Bones and gave an apologetic shrug. "We'll be right back."

He glanced at his chains, the faintest smile curling his mouth. "Go on, luv. I'll wait right here."

Seventeen

I'm not bargaining away my soul or anyone else's," were my first words when I followed Ian and the demon outside of the subterranean garage. Maybe if Balchezek thought I was uncompromising on this point, he wouldn't press me for conditions that, in my desperation, I might take him up on.

The demon snorted. "Good, because I don't want yours, and—newsflash—you don't have authority over anyone else's, Miss Overthinks Her Importance."

I was beyond relieved to hear that, but I pretended to bristle at the insult. Ian laughed. "She does at times, doesn't she?"

"Before we go further, why would you want to help vampires over your own kind?" I might be desperate, but I wasn't about to ignore the most logical question.

"Because I hate my job," Balchezek said promptly.

My brows rose. "You consider damning souls a *job*?"

"What would you call something you have to do in order to fit in, where you're bitched at whenever you underperform, yet you're never, ever appreciated for when you do it right?" Another snort. "I guess marriage also qualifies, but for me, it's contracting souls."

Was it possible that all demons weren't evil incarnate? That one could feel remorse over what he'd done? "So you don't like having to condemn people?"

He looked at me like I was crazy. "Some meat monkey comes crying to me about, oh, I need this or that, give it to me and you can have whatever you want. So I give it, then he bitches about the terms after the bill's come due, and *I'm* the one who's supposed to feel bad?"

All right, looked like I was wrong about him feeling remorse! "Yeah, because you're taking advantage of people when they're at their lowest," I pointed out. "It's not fair."

He rolled his eyes. "It's not like I was consulted when the downstairs went to war against the upstairs. I'm just supposed to do what I'm told, all day, every day, for the rest of eternity whether I like it or not. And if I don't do it, then I get thrown into the lake of fire. Don't talk to *me* about fair."

"So what do you want in return for helping us?" I asked, giving Balchezek a calculated once-over. "You're offering us information to help beat this demon, and you just proved that it's not out of a sense of repentance."

Balchezek smiled. "Not at all. I want a place in your world. If I try to abscond on my own, the higher-ups will come after me, and I'd rather die than get caught cowering among humans. But if I'm under a *vampire's* protection, I become more trouble than I'm worth. It's like I said, most demons don't want to poke the fang beehive if they can avoid it."

"You want me to take you in as a member of my line?" I couldn't quite keep the appalled sound out of my voice.

"You take in ghosts," he said, spitting out the word like it was foul. "Yet a demon isn't good enough for you? Besides, I don't want protection from *your* line. You're so priggish, you'd make me crazy. But you," a nod at Ian, "are more my style."

Ian inclined his head in acknowledgment of their similarities. "You're set in your decision? Because while I don't require morals from members of my line, I do expect loyalty. How can I be sure you won't change your mind later?"

"Know that movie where the underappreciated cubicle workers flip out, beat their copy machine to smithereens, and then rob their own company?" He flashed his teeth in something too feral to be considered a smile. "Consider that demon in your friend my copy machine, and my robbery is spilling secrets of my race to tell you how to save him, and your other friends, without killing them."

Ian stretched out his hand, which the demon grasped without hesitation. "Fulfill your promise, and you are welcome in my line with my full protection."

Balchezek shook his hand. "Great. That's part one of my terms."

Why wasn't I shocked that the demon had more conditions? "What's part two?"

He let go of Ian's hand and smiled at me. "Life's not worth living without a few basic comforts, eh? I want money. An obscene amount of money, to be specific."

I didn't have tons in the bank, but Bones had built up a fortune over his centuries of bounty hunting and investments guided by a vampire who caught glimpses of the future.

"Fine. When this is over, I'll be sure you get a check that'll make me vomit when I write it, how's that?"

Balchezek coughed. "I'll need a little down payment on that promise." And then he nodded at my hand.

I glanced down at the red diamond ring Bones had given me the day he asked me to marry him. Its sentimental value to me was priceless. Because of the rareness of red diamonds and its five-carat size, its market value was also through the roof.

I twisted it off and handed it over without needing a moment to think. I'd rather have Bones alive than a rock that would break my heart with memories if he were dead. "Fine. When you've helped us boot that bitch out of everyone without killing them, you'll give that back in exchange for your obscene check. Agreed?"

The creature who had bound countless others to supernatural deals stuffed the ring in his pocket and smiled. "Consider it done."

I smiled back, making sure to show my fangs in warning. "I'll hold you to that."

Two vampires and a demon, allied together. It was a Christmas miracle alright, but of the macabre kind. Still, I'd take my miracles however I could get them.

Eighteen

Balchezek said he needed to fact-check a few things and he'd return later, so it was only Ian and I who descended back into the underground garage.

"Tell me you did *not* barter your soul, Kitten," were Bones's first words when we came into sight.

Although I'd given that more than a passable thought, I was able to say, "Of course not," with total honesty. If I made sure to sound like I'd never even considered it, well, that was just the icing on the cake.

Bones drilled Ian with a hard stare next. "Is she lying?"

"You'd believe his word over mine?" I shook my head. "That's insulting."

Ian gave Bones a languid smile. "No worries, Crispin. Our sulfur-smelling mate has more pedestrian reimbursements in mind for any assistance he gives us."

"Really," I added when Bones still looked like he doubted we were telling the truth.

"We'll need to keep you chained until we hear from Balchezek and come up with a game plan," I went on, hating the necessity even as I acknowledged the reason for it. "Ian and I will watch over you in shifts. I'm sorry for the—"

"I'm not sorry," Bones cut me off. He'd been staring at me, but then he glanced away. "I can't harm you this way. That's all I bother about."

"Excuse us for a moment, Crispin," Ian said. Then he tugged me along to far side of the haphazard concrete maze where the hole to the outside was. He jumped out and I followed, wondering what was up now.

Ian walked over to the side of the street. "Are you trying to make Crispin lose the hold he has over the demon?"

I blinked at the question, too surprised to be offended. "Why would you say that?"

"He's shredded with guilt over what that demon made him do. Blimey, I'm a selfish conceited bastard and even I'd feel badly about kicking your face in and trying to kill you if you were my wife. Multiply that by Crispin's far finer qualities, and you have a man tormented. Yet you're acting as though he is to blame."

Okay, *now* I was angry. Didn't take long at all when talking to Ian. "I know it's not his fault. That it was all her, and he has nothing to feel bad about. So why don't you go take a flying fuck, Ian!"

"Why don't you take a chained one," he countered.

I scoffed. "I'm sure that's a fabulous British comeback, but it's wasted on me because I don't know what it means."

"It means," he replied, speaking slowly, as though I was a child, "that I've seen how you normally act after a separation where one of you was almost killed. You nearly kick people out of the way to shag each other. Yet all you're doing now is contributing to his guilt when you should be showing him that he's still the man you're in love with, demon or no demon. And chains or no chains."

My mouth opened, ready to let loose a caustic comment about how Ian thought sex fixed any situation, when I stopped. He might have a point. I could reassure Bones until I was blue in the face that I didn't consider him responsible for what the she-bitch did when she was in the driver's seat, but as the saying went, actions spoke louder than words. Granted, there was nothing romantic about an underground, abandoned Jiffy Lube station, but Bones had made more out of less when circumstances threw us a curve ball.

I'd just have to do the same.

"You don't get to stay and watch," was what I finally said.

His lips twitched. "It *would* be safer in case the demon resurged and took control—"

"Bite me," I cut him off.

This time, Ian didn't attempt to stuff back his laughter. "I'll leave that to Crispin."

Nineteen

An hour later, I jumped back down into the underground garage, winding through the support barriers until I reached the spot where Bones was secured. Ian reclined in front of him, one leg propped up on the pile of extra chains we had just in case.

I threw a hotel key card at Ian. We were checked in not far from there so we had another place to store our weapons.

"Here. Why don't you wash up, change clothes, and find someone to eat?" *And don't hurry back,* my pointed look added.

I'd already done two out of those three things, as my damp hair and new outfit attested. After all, I wasn't about to seduce my husband while his friend's scent still clung to me.

Ian rose. "Don't mind if I do. See you both in a bit."

I waited until I heard him exit before I set down the bag I'd been holding and began to arrange its contents on the floor.

Bones sniffed. "Scented candles?"

"I'm sick of the oil and blood smell," I responded, lighting them. "This is better."

I didn't need to look up to know his dark brown gaze followed my every movement. I could almost feel his stare, and though he tried to tamp down his aura, slivers of yearning and remorse whispered across my subconscious.

"Did Ian tell you that Balchezek says he knows another way to force the demon out without killing you and the others?" I asked, glancing at him.

His brows drew together. "Yes, but I don't trust demons."

I laughed, soft and wry. "I'm right there with you, but Balchezek has his reasons for helping us."

I wasn't going to repeat those reasons with the female demon eavesdropping inside Bones. Since possessing vampires was technically a demon no-no, I doubted the bitch could tattle on Balchezek without outing herself, but why give her an edge?

"You know what you have to do if he's wrong, Kitten."

The flatness in his voice made a shiver run through me that had nothing to do with the garage's frigid temperature. *Yeah. I'll find another way to save you,* I silently replied, but didn't say that out loud, either. Bones would only argue about promises and duty and I didn't care about any of those things if they meant he had to die.

I finished lighting the candles and walked over to him. His mouth was still set in a hard line, but his gaze raked over the contours of my body as though he couldn't stop himself. In addition to remorse and yearning, another emotion crested against my subconscious—possessiveness. He might know that I'd only had good intentions by my earlier actions with Ian, but his vampire nature demanded that he assert his claim over me. How well I knew that from being on the other side of the jealousy coin with Bones in the past.

"How's our demonic squatter?" I asked, brushing his chains.

"Angry." One word, clipped with the weight of emotions I felt him trying to hold back.

I smiled. "Good." Then I took out the key and unlocked the first of many bolts connecting his chains.

Tension slipped through the wall he'd erected around his aura. "What are you doing?"

I unwound a length of chain, letting it drop to the floor. "Making you more accessible. One down, half a dozen to go, and even then you'll still be unable to move your arms or legs."

"Don't." His eyes flashed green. "She's too dangerous."

I undid another section of chain before standing on tiptoe to slowly run my tongue down the side of his ear. "Fuck her," I whispered. "She's had you to herself too long, and you're *mine*."

More chains fell. His mouth brushed my cheek, control raging against the hunger I felt rising in him. "It's not safe," he tried again.

I laughed before I caught his ear with fangs that were already out from my growing desire. "Oh, Bones. How often do we ever play it safe?"

A low growl was my response. So was the blast of lust decimating the last of the barriers he'd had around his emotions. I reveled in both, licking the shell of his ear and then letting my breath tease the same space.

He couldn't grab me with his hands, but his aura enveloped me, sheathing me in a tingling cloud of power and raw need. It still felt fragmented from his fight to keep the demon down, but I had no doubt he would win that fight. Three more lengths of chain fell from around his waist. I could now reach through the remaining links and pull his shirt open, revealing the hard flesh of his chest and stomach.

"I missed you," I said, abandoning his ear for his lips.

His mouth closed over mine with such hunger that my embers of desire turned into a furnace. He didn't wait for me to part my lips, but invaded past them with deep, seeking strokes of his tongue. I moaned and tugged harder on his chains. More fell, until I could press my body against his and feel the bulge of something other than metal against me. He groaned, rough and guttural, when I reached down and clasped my hand around him.

His mouth tore away from mine, glowing green gaze pinning me in its intensity. "Take your clothes off. I need to see you."

I backed away on shaky legs, the roar of lust slamming into my subconscious making me almost glad he was chained. He felt wild, almost feral. Like he thought this was the last time we'd be together and he'd hold nothing back except the demon raging inside him. I drew the shirt over my head and tossed it aside, my skin rippling with gooseflesh under the rake of his gaze. My bra came off next, nipples already hard and aching. Then my jeans. I pulled my panties down with them, kicking both aside.

"Ravishing."

His accent was thicker, and he stared at me like he'd devour my flesh with his eyes. I stared back, absorbing the view of pale crystal flesh stretched over muscles that bunched and flexed against the chains. His features were almost frightening in their fierce beauty; mouth fuller from our recent kiss, eyes glittering green, jaw clenching from passionate impatience.

I was impatient, too, emotions surging in me that went well beyond lust. Someone was trying to steal away the most important person in the world to me, and I was going to take back what was mine. His gaze flared brighter when I stalked over, yanking away the last of the chains around his hips. A wealth of rigid flesh filled my hands when a rough tug split open the front of his jeans. Then I stepped on the discarded pile of metal to raise myself to his height, sliding my thigh up to his waist.

His mouth crushed over mine, tongue sensually ravaging me as he bent to bring that hard flesh against my center. I didn't have time to reach down to assist before a strong arch pushed him inside me, wringing a gasp from me that his mouth absorbed. Every nerve ending flared in welcome as another thrust brought him deeper, sending more pleasure searing through me. I gripped his shoulders through the chains when he moved again, burying himself to the hilt and then grinding against my clitoris in a way that sent spasms ricocheting through my loins.

I cried out when he did it again, locking my arms around his neck for leverage and hiking my other thigh up to press myself closer. He began to move in strong, measured strokes that had me begging for more in between kisses. Power slid along my back, curling around me to hold me aloft and molding my hips tighter against him than mere hands ever could. His thrusts intensified, sending aching currents of rapture through me. My head fell back and I leaned against that invisible grip, loins clenching in frenzied bliss with every deep, rapid stroke.

His throaty growls and my moans drowned out the clanking noises from the chains as we moved faster, faster, until I wasn't aware of anything except the overwhelming sensations surging inside me. They culminated in a climax that tore a hoarse shout from me, the feel of Bones's answering spasms sending more ecstatic ripples through my body.

Twenty

I sagged against him, feeling as though my arms and legs had been replaced with jelly. At some point, he'd knelt down as far as the chains allowed, so cold metal bit into my knees from my straddling him, but I didn't care. Everything still tingled too much for me to focus on the lack of comfortable surroundings.

"I don't want to move . . . ever," I managed.

His laugh was soft, wicked, and free of the concerns that bound him more securely than the chains lashing him to the support beam. Hearing it was another form of bliss, only this one reverberated deeper than even my previous, explosive climax.

Something soft touched my legs. I glanced down and saw a blanket winding its way up that had formerly been in the corner. Bones's power curled it higher, until it draped across my shoulders and warded away the chill in the air. Just further evidence that his will alone restrained him, rather than all the chains and locks Ian and I had wrapped around him.

"Show-off," I murmured, tucking it over both of us.

He smiled, but a shadow crossed his features, which I knew was the demon coming between us again. "I kept her from using that power as much as I could. If she takes me over once more, the chains will slow her enough for you to shoot me. Don't hesitate. You'll only have moments."

I didn't glance behind me to where we'd stacked the guns, but they were within easy reach. "I won't, but let's not talk about that now. You should try to get some sleep."

"No," he said at once. "She wants me to sleep so my resolve will be weakened and she can take me over again."

Anger burned through me, fueled by my love for Bones and the territorialism that was passed down from every vampire before me. This demon wasn't going to win. She was going to pay for picking my husband to possess. I'd chase her all the way to hell and back if that's what I had to do to get my revenge.

"Well, then she's got a long damn wait," I said, forcing my rage back enough to smile. "You rarely sleep as it is, and that's when you're *not* trying to squash a hell-bitch."

He touched his forehead to mine, closing his eyes. "You sleep, Kitten. You know I love holding you while you dream."

He couldn't touch me with his hands, but further waves of power cocooned me, somehow more intimate than flesh. I hated that he thought this might be the last time I fell asleep next to him, as the emotions brushing mine told me. With the demon lodged in him, Bones felt like every moment between us had an expiration date if he wanted to keep me safe. But I was equally stubborn about saving his life. This demon didn't know it yet, but she'd picked the *wrong* couple to fuck with.

I slid my arms around his neck, shifting until I was draped across his lap instead of straddling him. Then I closed my eyes, sighing as I got as comfortable as possible. I wasn't afraid to fall asleep next to him, demon-possessed or not. Nothing in this world or under it would make Bones drop his guard and endanger me while I was vulnerable.

"I love you," I whispered, tucking my head under his chin.

Something teased at my subconscious right as I felt myself drift off. Balchezek, talking about the intricacies of simultaneous possession of vampires. *The upside is*

that if you pull it off, you're not limited to only possess-
ing your anchor's human family. You could also go up
to the third or fourth generation of your anchor's siring
bloodline. . .

Wraith was the female demon's anchor, but that
meant she should only have been able to possess *Bones*
first. Once in Bones, she could have split off into the
other vampires when they fell asleep; everyone at the
cabin except Denise was within the required first four
generations of the same vampiric bloodline. But it
wasn't Bones that the demon had mutilated in that hotel
room in order to force her first simultaneous possession. That had been Annette, yet Wraith and Annette
weren't related as he and Bones were, so that shouldn't
have been possible, unless. . .

I bolted upright, startling Bones. "What?" he demanded.

"Bones. I— I think Annette might be the person
who changed Wraith into a vampire two centuries ago."

The sun was just starting to set when Balchezek suddenly appeared in our underground hideout.

"Got some news," he announced. He might dispar-
age ghosts, but he had a lot in common with them when
it came to unexpected entrances. "Let's talk topside so
we can have some privacy."

"Go," Bones said when I hesitated, hating the need to treat him this way because of the enemy inside him. But I pushed that back and threw on some clothes, then met Balchezek outside by the side of the road, where it was impossible for Bones to overhear us. Ian was there, too, eyeing the demon expectantly.

"I did some digging about how you boot the demon from your pals," Balchezek started. "I was right! There is a way aside from the bone-knife-to-the-eyes approach, and the only person who has to die is the demon's main anchor."

"Wraith," I said, feeling torn. "We'd have to kill Wraith?"

Balchezek beamed. "Who's your favorite demon, huh? Told you I'd earn the revoltingly high check you're going to give me."

"But you said before that you could save Bones and all the others without killing them," I reminded him.

"Yeah, your other *friends*." A shrug. "Didn't think you considered Wraith your friend."

"I don't, but if he's possessed, an innocent man who happens to be my husband's brother is still in there somewhere," I replied sharply.

Balchezek sighed. "If you believe in the naïve idea that *anyone's* innocent, then that's true. Look, I hate to use a cliché, but you can't make an omelet without breaking some eggs, okay? You have to choose between the lives of all your friends or the life of one stranger you just happen to be related to."

I said nothing, but my jaw clenched, the only outward sign of the roiling emotions that crested through me.

"If it helps, I doubt he has much personality left," Balchezek went on. "I told you that Hazael would've had to possess her anchor when he was still human. How long do you think your boy has been a vampire? Because that's how long he's been possessed. Probably a vegetable by now." A shrug. "Like I said, if your kind were easy to squat inside, my people wouldn't be afraid of ruffling your feathers. We'd have taken you over millennia ago instead."

Two centuries of being possessed. Even if Wraith did have any consciousness left, he must be a madman after having his will hijacked that long. No one's sanity could endure that much stress.

"If it's the only way to save the others, then Wraith dies," Ian stated.

I wanted to disagree, to find another way, because it was awful enough to sentence an innocent man to die for the greater good, but even worse when that man was the brother Bones never knew. Yet I said nothing, and my silence confirmed my acceptance.

I was glad we couldn't tell Bones this. He'd think we were withholding information because we didn't want the demon in him overhearing our plots, but I didn't want Bones to carry the guilt over it. He'd taken vengeance against my father so I wouldn't have to. The least I could do was carry the sin of his brother's blood on my hands versus his. I might not like sacrificing Wraith's life, but if it was a choice between him or Bones, that was no choice to me.

And the demon didn't seem to realize it, but he'd revealed another important detail. I exchanged a glance with Ian, who nodded almost imperceptibly. He'd caught it, too.

"When do we strike?" I asked.

"Have to wait until mid-December," Balchezek replied.

"No way. She knows we're onto her. Why would we give her another two weeks to plot against us?"

"How many times do I have to tell you I don't make the rules?" Balchezek grumbled. "Mid-December is when many of the world's largest religions begin their big to-do's. Christmas, Hanukkah, Winter Solstice, Muharram . . . faith is at an all-time high. That weakens demons. If you want to drive those splits out of your pals, that's when you have your best shot."

"If she knows she'll be weaker soon, what's to stop her from killing everyone before that happens? That's what I would do," Ian stated with blunt callousness.

"Survival instinct," the demon replied. He jerked his head at me. "Know how your vampire grabbed control instead of killing her, or watching you sex her up? What do you think will happen if the demon tries to kill the people those other vampires care about? She'll have a mass uprising, that's what. So until she's got everything in place, she'll keep those vamps complacent by not fucking with who they love."

Everything in place. For the demon, that would be her assurance of taking over Bones's line when he died. He'd publicly disowned me, but if needed, we could reverse that and deal with the consequences of his enemies and people knowing they had no head to their line. Plus, as long as we had Bones, then the demon couldn't act against the others yet. She'd need them if she tried to find another way to grab the same power. We would use her own plan against the bitch.

"All right, then it's mid-December." My smile was tight. "So we have to kill Wraith, which we know how to do. But how do we get the demon's splits out of Bones and the others?"

Balchezek laced his hands behind his head. "That's where your filmy little friends come in."

Twenty-One

Two weeks before Christmas, Fabian flew into our new location in a derelict waterfront factory with the news we'd been waiting for.

"Denise picked up the charges and she is on the boat."

"Thank God she managed to get away," I breathed. "How'd she do it?"

"Wraith would not consent to let her leave no matter what excuse she fabricated, so Denise turned herself into a duplicate of your cat and meowed at the door until one of them let her outside. They never knew it was her."

Faint wonder tinged Fabian's voice at Denise's shapeshifting ability. It still bowled me over, too, and I'd seen her do it several times.

Ian chuckled. "Clever poppet."

I was too keyed up to comment on Denise's smart improvisation. Bones was below in the former boiler room, slumped in his chains, locked in a battle of wills against a creature that could be thousands of years old. So much of his willpower focused on his internal struggle that he couldn't spare the energy to stand. Fifteen days of this while not allowing himself a moment of sleep had taken a brutal toll.

It had tormented me to watch the demon eat him up from the inside out while not being able to help, but finally, I could act. Not a moment too soon, either. Even with his extraordinary willpower, I didn't think Bones could make it much longer.

"Then let's get this show on the road," I stated. "Fabian, you know what to do. Ian, summon Balchezek. I'll get Bones."

I went downstairs, my heart clenching when I saw his dark head bent forward on his chest. His eyes were closed, and not a muscle twitched on his tall frame. Inwardly, I sighed. He'd fallen asleep. I knew it would happen soon. It had been a miracle that he'd held out this long, especially since Bones had no idea that we were waiting for a specific date to act. How could we tell him when that would only be alerting the demon, too? He'd been fighting with no end in sight, and his body had at last given out.

Well, maybe we'd be lucky and he'd sleep so long that we'd have the demon beaten before he woke up and she took over—

His eyes opened, startling me. They settled on me in what looked like an unfocused manner.

"Kitten?"

"Bones?" I replied with the same amount of question in my voice.

"Mmm." That was his only response, as if more words were too much for him.

Was it still him? He might have had his eyes closed for concentration; I'd seen him do that before. But in his current state, I'd be amazed if he could shut his eyes and *not* sleep. Or had he been asleep and this was the demon pretending to be exhausted so I'd think Bones was still at the forefront?

I had to be sure. "What was the first thing I said to you when we met?" The demon had infected his body, but Bones had confirmed that she didn't have access to his memories, just like he knew almost nothing about her.

He didn't reply, just kept staring at me with that unfocused look in his eyes. I shook his shoulder roughly, chains rattling under my touch.

"Come on, Bones! What was the first thing I said to you when we met?"

Even as I spoke, I drew my gun out of my pants. I kept one on me at all times now, knowing it was only a matter of time until I had to shoot him.

"Hallo handsome," he mumbled. "Want to fuck?"

Relief coursed through me and I put my gun back in its holster. Those were the words I'd said when I was an inexperienced vampire hunter looking to entice Bones outside so I could kill him. What I'd lacked in charm I made up for in bluntness.

"You have to hang on a little longer," I told him as I began to unwind the chains that tethered him to several pipes. "We're moving to another location."

"Kitten, I can't . . . do this anymore."

The words sliced through me like a dozen silver blades. He sounded so awful that all I wanted to do was cradle him while he slept for three straight days. This was too much. I wouldn't have held out half this long. It was horrible to ask anything else of him, but even though it was unfair, I had to push all my tender feelings aside.

"You need to do this," I said sharply. "We're not safe here and we need to leave. Don't you dare fall asleep and let her attack us now. I thought you loved me."

I hated myself for every word. If I were Bones, I'd tell me to fuck off and then I'd start snoring. But he shook his head as if to clear it and then somehow forced himself to stand even with hundreds of pounds of chains coiled around him.

I'd never loved him more—or been more determined to boot that she-bitch inside him back to hell. "That's right," I went on while mentally promising to make this up to him. "Stay alert."

I kept up a steady stream of conversation that only a drill sergeant would consider encouraging as I removed most of the chains but kept his arms locked to his chest in a metallic version of a straightjacket. Then I stuck some earphones in his ears and put a black hood over his face with a final brusque admonition for him to stay focused. *Heartless bitch, table for one!* I thought, but if things went according to plan, he'd be free of the demon tonight. As my last step of preparation, I duct-taped an iPod to his chains and turned it up. Loudly.

Thus blinded and deafened, I led him up the stairs to the first floor. It would have been quicker if I carried him, but an abrupt "no" from under the hood stopped me when I started to lift him. Male pride survived even a fortnight's lack of sleep and a demon's merciless assault, it seemed. That was fine. Bones could be cursing me up one side and down the other as an ungrateful bitch, and if it gave him strength, I'd cheer him on.

Ian stood next to a bloody series of symbols, Balchezek on the other side of them. Good to know he still responded promptly to his supernatural pages. A plastic container the size of a purse was at the demon's feet, and he hefted it with a smile.

"All right, fangers. Let's put the baby in your friends to bed!"

My thoughts exactly.

Very few people were in this derelict section of town, which was good. If anyone saw us leading a hooded, chained man to the car, they'd call the police and report a kidnapping. But, thankfully, no one stopped us as we sped off toward Ocean Isle Beach, where a boat waited for us on the stormy waters of the North Carolina coast.

Twenty-Two

Waves bounced our boat like a stone skipping across a pond as we made our way toward the small craft bobbing in the distance. With my enhanced vision, I made out Denise's dark head at the helm, the wind whipping her hair into Medusa-like tendrils. I slowed our craft to idle speed, letting the current direct us instead of the speedboat's powerful engines. We didn't want to get too close. Denise made no move to approach us, either. She kept her craft where it was, staying as still as a statue in her position by the wheel.

Less than an hour later, I heard the roar of another engine coming from the direction of the harbor. With darkness approaching, the frigid temperatures, and small-craft advisory warnings, I didn't think it was a family out for a pleasure cruise. A sleek white craft cleaved through the water toward Denise's boat, the sun's dying rays illuminating the pale hair of the vampire at that helm.

A vampire who bore a striking resemblance to Bones.

"If you wanted to escape me, you should have paid in cash instead of using your credit card to rent your boat!" Wraith shouted at Denise. His voice carried over the waters to us, sounding feminine and bearing no trace of an English accent. He barely glanced in our direction, though he had to notice us drifting less than a quarter-mile away. For Wraith to be so unconcerned, he must not be alone in the boat.

To prove my guess, I next saw a blond head appear, then three brunets, and finally, a strawberry blonde. Looked like Wraith brought the whole crew with him. I didn't think he'd risk leaving them unattended after we'd snatched Bones out from under him. But when the Egyptian vampire turned in our direction, I tensed. With the distance and the way both our crafts rocked on the waves, I'd never get a clear head shot on him, but Mencheres's powers didn't need a calm surface or closer proximity to be effective.

"Now," I barked into my cell phone.

Three things happened at once. Ghosts shot out of the bottom of my boat, winding through me, Ian, and

Bones in such great number that our bodies were engulfed in their diaphanous forms. At that same time, the instant crushing pressure I'd felt on my neck muted to only a strangling sensation that was unpleasant but not lethal, since I didn't need to breathe.

And Denise's boat blew up with a spectacular explosion.

The *boom* followed by debris shooting out in every direction claimed Wraith's full attention. He tried to turn his boat around, but he'd been too close to Denise's craft when it blew. Flaming pieces of wreckage showered down onto him and the other vampires, some bits pelting through the side of Wrath's craft from their velocity. That pressure around my neck lessened even more.

"Kitten!" Bones shouted, his aura surging with what felt like a shot of adrenaline.

Ian yanked the hood off him and began to undo his chains.

"Get ready. It's time to reclaim our mates," Ian said with vicious satisfaction.

With an equally ruthless grin, I gunned the throttle on the speedboat and headed straight toward Wraith's vessel. He continued to try to clear the dangerous pieces of wreckage from his boat, cursing at the damage the nearby explosion had done. We were a hundred yards away before Wraith seemed to realize that we weren't slowing down.

Through the hazy layer of ghosts still twining all over me, making my whole body feel electrified, I saw realization dawn on Wraith's face.

"Stop them! Kill them!" he screamed at Mencheres. Then he abandoned his attempts at clean-up and swung the boat around, gunning his engine.

It sputtered, sounding like something was caught in the jets or they'd been damaged from the explosion. Our craft also began to shake, but Fabian and Elisabeth had brought a lot of their kind with them. More ghosts appeared, gloving the craft with their bodies and acting as a supernatural buffer against Mencheres's power.

The former pharaoh's abilities were staggering, but they didn't work on anything from the grave. Silly me had needed a demon to remind me of that. Balchezek and others might mock me for my affinity for ghosts, but with their bodies acting as a force field to deflect Mencheres's formidable power, it was good to have friends in dead places.

Ian got the last of the chains off Bones and threw them aside. "When you hit the water, swallow enough to rupture your stomach, and then keep swallowing," I said urgently, glancing at him. "All that salt water will make it easier to purge the bitch out of you."

Bones reached out and pulled me to him for a fierce kiss. Ghosts still swirled around and through us, but it was the touch of his hands—the first I'd felt of them in weeks—that made my body vibrate.

Balchezek shoved himself between us, muttering, "No time." I glanced at how close we were to Wraith's boat. He was right.

"We're coming for you, motherfucker!" I shouted at the demon inhabiting my husband and friends. Our speedboat struck Wraith's craft before my words had died away.

The impact catapulted us out of the boat. Bones sank immediately beneath the waves, but Ian flew straight up, taking Balchezek with him. I had a different agenda. I dove through the raining pieces of two decimated boats, ghosts still clinging to me, to snatch a blond vampire up before she hit the water.

"Mencheres!" I roared, holding a struggling Kira in my grip. "Pull yourself on top of that demon inside you or I swear I'll kill her!"

So saying, I rammed a silver knife into Kira's chest, careful to be close to her heart without actually piercing it. Kira stilled as though she'd been flash-frozen, emitting a hoarse noise of pain that I more sensed than heard above the hissing and sputtering from the two sinking crafts.

A black head breached the waves, bright green gaze leveled on me with a look that was truly frightening.

"If you let that bitch even splash me with your power, she dies," I warned him again, staring right back at Mencheres.

Come on, I silently urged. Out of the corner of my eye, I saw Wraith scrabble onto an overturned piece of hull, but he didn't try to interfere. Not with his body, anyway. I could almost feel the demonic energy roiling off him toward Mencheres. The demon didn't want to lose his most powerful puppet.

Another vampire vaulted out of the water at me, but before Spade reached me, Ian caught him in a midair tackle that tumbled them both out of my range of vision.

"Watch the water!" Balchezek snapped, not being shielded from its damaging effects because he was a corporeal demon. Not wearing someone else's body like Wraith.

I didn't dare turn my attention from Mencheres. Currents of energy crackled around him, and if not for the thick blanket of ghosts cocooning me, I knew I'd be missing my head.

I yanked the knife a little higher, causing Kira to cry out again, and something snapped in Mencheres's expression. For a split-second, I thought that not even the myriad of ghosts could save me, but then I felt him drawing *in* those deadly currents of energy instead of snapping them outward at me. Wraith let out a howl that sounded pained.

"Cat." Mencheres's voice was ragged. "It is I. Let her go."

"Prove it. Force Spade and Annette underwater and make them drink salt water until it's flooding them," I said.

"No!" Wraith shouted, surging toward me.

A wall of power swatted him back into the upturned remains of the hull hard enough to crack its surface—and Wraith's skull. Blood poured out onto the white underside before disappearing into the ocean. Wraith groaned in a higher-pitched, feminine voice.

Then I heard a splash. Heard Ian's muttered, "Drink up, mates," and guessed that Spade and Annette had just been shoved underwater. All these were promising signs, but I still kept that knife jammed into Kira's chest. The demon had to be fighting Mencheres tooth and nail, and nothing would motivate the vampire to keep control like fear for his lover's life.

Of course, when this was all over, Mencheres might still kill me for stabbing Kira.

"Bring me to him . . . carefully!" Balchezek snapped.

Ian descended to where Wraith was with the demon still tucked under his arm like a large football. When

Wraith saw them, he tried to slip back into the ocean to get away.

"Hold him still," I told Mencheres curtly.

Power lashed out, pinning Wraith to the upturned hull. Ian adjusted his grip on Balchezek, holding him by the waist so the demon dangled above the trapped vampire with his arms free. Balchezek gave Wraith a cheery smile before ripping his shirt open, exposing the vampire's pale, firm chest.

Wraith screamed something in a language I didn't understand when Balchezek plucked a knife from his belt and began carving symbols onto Wraith's chest. Instead of those symbols vanishing from instant healing, the waves seemed to set them in place, emblazoning the symbols on his skin. The demon was so deeply lodged inside Wraith that his open wounds reacted to the salt water the same way a vampire's did to liquid silver.

"Burns, doesn't it?" Balchezek remarked over the feminine-sounding shrieks that were like music to my ears. *Take that, bitch!* I felt like crowing.

"How dare you betray one of your own for *them?*" Wraith snarled, in English this time.

Balchezek didn't pause in his carving. "Easy. I'm getting a lot of money. Imagine that; a demon without a conscience."

His knife flashed again, and Kira shuddered in my arms. I would've thought it was pain from the knife I still had lodged in her, except I saw Mencheres do the same thing.

"Almost done," Balchezek muttered, carving faster. Kira's shuddering increased until I worried that the tremors would edge the knife too close to her heart. Mencheres continued to be affected the same way, too. The waters around him began to froth.

"Almost," Balchezek said again, the knife now flashing so fast that it was nearly a blur. "There!" he announced.

That single word was accompanied by a blast that felt stronger than when the boat detonated, only this didn't shoot off in several directions. All that invisible trajectory was aimed at Wraith, interrupting even Mencheres's iron hold to briefly bow Wraith's body under the weight of its onslaught. For a second, I thought it might blow him to pieces.

But then that energy abruptly dissipated. Wraith slumped before Mencheres's grip immobilized him again. In between the various floating pieces of boat debris around us, Bones's head broke the surface. Though he still looked exhausted, the smile he flashed me was filled with immeasurable satisfaction.

"She's gone," he said simply.

Twenty-Three

Even though the symbols Balchezek carved reversed the original ritual and sent the demon splits out of everyone else and back into Wraith, Mencheres and Kira still drank enough salt water to kill a normal person from organ rupture. The goal was to have everyone's bodies filled with the liquid so they would be inhospitable to demonic repossession, because we weren't done yet.

Denise swam over in time to be enveloped in a bear hug from a newly un-possessed Spade. She'd jumped off the boat before detonating it, but her top looked ragged and lacerations crisscrossed her face from being in the blast radius. At least with her nearly immortal status, she'd be healed in hours.

Ian still held Balchezek aloft. The demon's skin looked red and irritated from the residual sea spray, but he'd stayed out of the ocean for more reasons than how the salt water would burn him. Balchezek tore away some of the duct tape that had kept the rectangular plastic container secured to his belt and opened the latch, pulling out a large rat. The rodent's rapid heartbeat was audible even above the sound of the waves.

Balchezek grinned at Wraith. "Look at your new home," he said while holding the rat above the vampire's stricken face. Mencheres still had Wraith in a punishing squeeze of power, cutting off even his ability to speak.

"Don't torment the creature," I snapped, flying over.

Balchezek snorted. "Now you feel bad for the demon?"

"I was talking about the rat," I said. "Give it to me."

Balchezek handed the rodent to me with a muttered comment about misguided feminine sappiness.

"Will drinking enough salt water force the demon out of him and into that?" Bones asked, nodding at the rat.

I briefly closed my eyes. I'd hoped to have this part done before Bones resurfaced so it would be too late for him to be involved, but I hadn't had the chance.

And now I had to tell him the truth.

"Wraith can't be saved." I wished he could tap into my feelings to know how sorry I was about this, but his emotional connection as the vampire who sired me only went one way. "The demon is in him so deep; she couldn't pull herself out if she wanted to. The only way to get her out of him is to kill him."

Pain brushed over my emotions, mixed with a jaded resignation that I hated because I'd felt it too often from Bones. Life had been cruel to him many times in the past, and it seemed Fate wasn't done with her tricks yet.

"I suspected as much, but . . . I'd hoped."

Those quiet words broke my heart. I came over, pulling out a silver knife with grim resolve. Better for Bones and the man trapped underneath the demon inhabiting him to make this quick.

I nodded at Ian. "Now."

Ian abruptly plunged into the ocean, forcing Balchezek down with him. Water covered Balchezek up to his waist, and he screamed like he'd been plunged into acid.

"Get me out of this!"

"Not so fast," I said coolly. "Why don't you tell us the *real* reason you've been helping us trap this demon?"

"Because you're fucking paying me!" Balchezek thundered, the words ending on another anguished yowl.

I watched his skin bubble up without mercy. The salt water wouldn't kill him, but it might make him wish he were dead. "Liar. You slipped up and called her Hazael, but none of us knew her name, and you didn't admit to recognizing her even though you obviously did. So let's try this again. Why did you really help us?"

Balchezek glared at me as the water looked like it boiled around him. I stared back, unblinking. "Go on, take your time. I love a nice evening swim in the ocean."

"She's my ticket to a better job," he gritted out.

My brows rose. "I thought you wanted Ian's protection because you were quitting that job."

"And live the rest of my life among fangers?" The skin on his face began to split, but he smiled even though that made it worse. "I'd rather stay in this ocean. No, I'm earning my way out of the minor leagues, and bringing in Hazael will guarantee my promotion."

"So you were going to let us do all the legwork whilst you made off with the prize?" Bones let out a derisive snort. "Right piece of work you are. Why is Hazael worth so much to your kind that she'd guarantee you a promotion?"

Another grotesque smile. "You know America's Most Wanted list? Demons have their own version, and Hazael's been on it for over two centuries. Probably why she jumped into a human to hide. She must've thought she hit the jackpot when that human got turned into a vampire; I told you demons avoid the vampire world as a rule. But just like greed and arrogance led her to kill an influential Fallen, Hazael must've gotten fed up living the quiet life inside the vampire she'd possessed. Maybe she thought enough time had passed that she could risk expanding her powers without getting caught. So she went for the simultaneous possessions and grab for Mastership of your lines. Probably had even bigger plans after she got them."

I nodded at Ian, who pulled Balchezek out of the water. Enough of it soaked his clothes so he wouldn't be able to dematerialize, but that also meant his skin still looked like it was being cooked.

"I've got good news and bad news. The good news is that I'm honoring our agreement and I'll let you go with a fat check for your help getting Hazael out of our friends. The bad news is that's all you're getting, because you're not taking her with you."

Then I handed the squirming rat to Spade, who took it with a distasteful expression.

"I need you to fly this thing at least a mile away."

Spade had dealt with demons before, so he flew off without questioning the directive. No other boats were around, so, in a few moments, there would be nothing else available for Hazael to jump into once she was forced out of Wraith. Ian and I had our warding tattoos, Denise's brands made her scorched earth to a demon, and all the other vampires and marine life in the near vicinity were filled with salt water.

There would be only one place Hazael could go—straight down to the fiery pit, and no demon I'd ever heard of went there willingly. It was the one place every demon seemed to truly fear.

Balchezek began to struggle. "You can't do this to me. I already told my boss that I would come back with her!"

"Then you should have made that part of our deal instead of lying," I replied coldly. "You know the old saying. Don't bitch about the terms after the bill's come due."

The demon shot me a dirty look at my paraphrasing of his former words, but then quit struggling when Ian pulled out the bone knife and held it near Balchezek's eyes.

"Don't make me use this, I still quite like you."

He continued to glare at me, but now stayed silent and complacent. I met Bones's gaze and curled my hand tighter around the silver knife. "Let me handle this," I said low.

He looked at the vampire that was his brother. From Wraith's widened eyes, I could tell the demon inside him was struggling with all her might to get free, but Mencheres's power was too strong for Hazael. Considering the scent of anger that was palpable even with Mencheres floating in the ocean, he wasn't the slightest bit conflicted about ending Wraith's life if it meant harming the demon who'd controlled him for weeks.

Then Bones looked back at me and his mouth twisted. "No, luv. He's the last of my family. It's my responsibility to do this one final deed for him."

He took the knife from me, staring into Wraith's vivid blue eyes as he waded through the water to him and then set the tip against Wraith's exposed chest.

"If underneath her you can hear me at all, brother," Bones said softly, "know that I am truly sorry I never knew you."

Then he shoved the blade down to its hilt. A hard, efficient twist, first to the left, then the right, extinguished the light in Wraith's eyes. Very slowly, the vampire's skin began to shrivel as true death started the aging process that had been delayed hundreds of years.

And right after that, a roar filled the air, sounding as though it came from everywhere and nowhere at the same time. The wind coming from it stank like sulfur and blasted the wet hair back from my face. It increased, whipping the waves to white caps and chasing away the ghosts that had lingered around us. My eyes stung from the bitter gale and the growing shrieks made my head throb, but the demon still wasn't done. Pressure built until it felt like my insides would pop from the strain.

But I wasn't afraid. I knew what this was—Hazael's last moments on earth, and I shouted into that indistinct whirlwind with all the anger left in me.

"Say hi to hell for me, bitch!"

That disembodied howl grew to a thunderous crescendo, exploding my eardrums. A blast of power hit me with the effect of a swinging wrecking ball. But then, abrupt as a lightning bolt, there was nothing but silence. The wind and pressure vanished, the seas around us ceased their frothing, and though I felt blood trickling out of my ears, I smiled. My eardrums would soon heal, and thinking about what Hazael was going through now made that small pain feel sweet.

Bones swam closer to wrap his arms around me. "You all right, Kitten?"

His voice sounded faint from my still-healing ears, but I leaned into his arms with a profound sense of relief. Everything was all right now.

"You can let Balchezek go," I told Ian. Then, to the demon, I said, "You'll get your check when I get my ring back."

Twenty-Four

Bones fell asleep during the car ride back to the cabin. He slept all through the night while I stripped both houses of everything that smelled like his brother, down to throwing away the rug that had hidden the symbols for the ritual that split Hazael into several different parts. The others were glad to help in this endeavor, and before dawn broke, the only evidence that Wraith had ever been here was the sheet-draped portrait of the Duke of Rutland and a box containing the Russell ancestral records. Wraith's remains were buried on the lower section of the hill, marked with a wooden cross that had a warding spell etched onto it. It was the best way I knew to ensure he rested in peace.

Ian and I also answered everyone's questions as to how their possessions had been possible, and why he, I, and Denise had remained unscathed. We left out only one detail, but I was waiting for Bones to wake up before going into that. I showed off my new warding tattoo, since it was on my hip and I didn't need to see Ian take his pants off again. Though the chances of any other possessed-human-turned-vampire wreaking havoc in our line were incalculably slim, I saw matching warding tattoos in everyone's near future. Better safe than sorry.

Then, shortly after dawn, I fell into bed next to my husband. Bones didn't move, but tendrils of power curled around me, showing some part of him was aware of my presence even if the rest of him was out cold. I didn't expect him to wake up until that evening at least, so I was startled when, only a few hours later, I awoke to the sound of Bones's raised voice.

" . . . explain *how* you could have kept such a thing from me!"

Uh-oh. I hurried downstairs to find Annette seated on the couch with Bones pacing in front of her. She was in a nightgown and he still wore the same salt-stiffened clothes he'd fallen asleep in, so Bones must have woken up and then immediately dragged her out of bed. Considering the topic, I couldn't blame him for his impatience.

"You knew I had a brother." His finger stabbed the air near her as he spoke. "You knew because you turned him into a vampire, else the demon in Wraith couldn't have split off into you first. So I ask again why you never revealed this to me in the two hundred and twenty years that we've known each other!"

Now I wasn't the only one awakened by Bones's strident voice. Ian came into the living room, and I heard low mutterings behind Spade and Denise's door. Kira and Mencheres were in the other cabin, but if Bones kept this up, he'd wake them, too.

Annette took in a deep breath, a spasm of pain crossing her features. "Because while I was still human, I swore an oath that I would never tell you about your father's family."

His gaze was harder than flint. "Who did you swear this oath to? Who was this person you valued more than everything I've ever done for you?"

She met his stare. "She was Lucille, your mother's half-cousin . . . and the madam of the bordello you grew up in."

My eyes widened. According to what Bones had told me years ago, Lucille was also the person responsible for him turning into a gigolo when he was seventeen.

"His second cousin was a she-pimp for both Bones *and* his mother?" I asked Annette in disbelief.

"You make it sound so crude," Annette muttered. "You have no idea what it was like to be impoverished in the seventeen hundreds. There was no welfare, no food stamps, and no opportunities. When Penelope's father took the Duke of Rutland's money and then turned her out into the street, Lucille was the only one who took her in. Could she help it that the only means she had to assist Penelope was by offering the same employment she herself endured? The same was true when Crispin was older."

"Mind your tone with my wife," Bones said sharply, but I'd felt the emotions cresting in him. Poignant sparks of remembrance told me Annette's bleak assessment had been correct. What sounded like coldness when filtered through my modern, privileged viewpoint had perhaps been kindness back then.

"I found out all this after you were arrested for stealing," Annette continued on, her voice husky now. "Lucille was far from flawless, but she did love you. She knew of my affection for you, too, so she came to me, told me the story of your parentage, and begged me to contact the Duke of Rutland regarding your predicament. He'd never disputed that he was the father of Penelope's babe, so Lucille thought he might intercede on your behalf. If he didn't, you'd surely hang."

Annette closed her eyes, running a hand through her golden-red hair. "I arranged for a private audience with the duke, though I confess I wondered if Lucille was mad. That changed the moment he walked into the room. You saw the portrait, Crispin, so you know how closely you resemble him. I relayed your circumstances and begged him to intercede with the judge, but he refused. He said he had only one son, his new, legitimate heir, and then he turned me out."

I now understood why Annette hadn't ever wanted to tell Bones this part of his history. My dad had also been a prick, and while I didn't begrudge anyone a happy relationship with their father, sometimes I felt a wistful sense of loss hearing others speak of a bond I'd never have.

Annette glanced away. "You already know I sought the judge out myself and persuaded him to deport you to the colonies instead of sentencing you to the rope. When I went back to Lucille and informed her of everything, she made me swear that should you ever return, I would never reveal your father's identity or actions to you. And so I swore on your life not to do so." A tear slipped down her cheek. "Nothing else would have held me to that promise for so long, Crispin."

Now I couldn't feel anything from Bones. He'd locked his emotions behind an impregnable wall. "What of Wraith?"

She sighed. "I kept tabs on him during the nearly twenty years that you were away. He seemed a decent lad. Then, a few years after you turned me, I heard that he'd become involved in a secret noblemen's sect that sought power through the occult. I returned to London without you and confirmed it was true. Your father was dead by then, as was the duke's younger brother and Wraith's mother, so he had no family left except you. I thought . . . I thought by informing Wraith about vampires, perhaps he'd turn from the occult in favor of undead powers. So I showed him what I was and told him of you. He seemed terribly excited and was determined to meet you as a new vampire. Only now do I realize I may have been speaking to the demon instead of him."

"And you changed him over." Bones's voice was flat.

"Yes." Spoken as she met his gaze again. "After he was past the blood craze, I was going to introduce him as your birthday present and pretend to have accidentally discovered your familial connection by hearing his true name. But when I arrived at his house that day, I found a note saying he couldn't bear what he'd become and he was ending his own life. I searched the grounds and found a burned corpse with a silver knife in its chest. I believed it to be him, and felt it was my punishment for intending to break the vow I'd made to Lucille not to involve you with your father's family."

Annette let out a short laugh. "Two hundred years later, I received a call from a man claiming to be

Wraith and saying he was ready to meet his brother as his birthday present. I didn't believe it, but I hadn't told anyone about him. So I waited at the hotel instead of leaving with Ian and the others, and, well, you know what happened then."

Yeah. Hazael showed up wearing Wraith's body like a Trojan horse and bled Annette enough to force the demon's first possession split into her. If not for Ian's horniness, we would never have known that she'd been attacked, and I would have had a lot less reason to be suspicious of Wraith at first.

"I don't expect you to forgive me, Crispin," Annette said, swiping away the moisture from her earlier tear. Her voice became brisk. "I await your punishment."

I personally thought Annette had been punished enough by holding those secrets for over two hundred years. Any sins she was guilty of were committed out of love and her own sense of honor, which might not be the same as mine, but it was just as sincere. Still, I wasn't her sire, so the decision wasn't mine.

Bones's mouth twisted. "What shall I do? Beat you? Cut you off from my line? With your knowledge of my past and my family, you are the only link that I have left to them."

"Actually," Ian said, speaking for the first time since he'd come in the room, "that's not quite true."

Epilogue

Christmas Eve

Even with the additional leafs added to my dining-room table, we still had to squeeze together to make room for everyone. Only one out of the eleven people here ate food for sustenance, but the table was piled high with all the traditional fixings, and everyone corporeal pretended to be hungry for it.

Bones carved the turkey while the rest of us heaped our plates with side dishes. I would have been happy to cook, but oddly enough—and I refused to acknowledge that it might have to do with my culinary skills—everyone insisted on bringing something. Bones roasted the turkey, Kira made the dressing, Denise baked the pies, Mencheres made a Middle Eastern dish that I didn't recognize, Spade provided the mashed potatoes, Annette candied the yams, my mother baked the green bean casserole, and Ian brought the wine.

I felt one person's absence acutely today. My uncle and I still weren't on speaking terms, but I was glad that my mother was here, spooning dressing onto her plate before passing the container to Denise. Fabian and Elisabeth were here as well, floating above the two chairs we'd left open for them. After all, they were as important to me as everyone else at the table. They just didn't take up as much physical space.

I tapped my wineglass with a fork, the dinging noise getting everyone's attention. "I'd like to propose a toast," I said, rising and lifting my glass. "To family, whether by blood or by affection. We'd all be lesser people without them."

Multiple glasses clinked together, but before I could sit down, Ian spoke.

"Another toast, this one to the Honorable Viscount Maynard. Though you were a sod who didn't help your sister Penelope when she was thrown out by her da, at least you were a randy bloke who shagged your serving girl or I wouldn't have been born."

"Here, here," Bones said, grinning as he clicked glasses with Ian.

Now I knew why Ian had looked so shocked when Bones revealed that his mother was really Penelope